Outlaws?

Bobby Joe looked out the window and nearly stopped breathing. Five men, their faces covered with bandannas, were riding toward them with guns drawn.

"Get down!" he ordered as he put his arm around Susannah and pulled her down himself.

"Oh, dear!" Nigel murmured up above them. When Bobby Joe realized that the elderly man was frozen in fright, he grabbed him by the front of his shirt and pulled him down, too.

"What. . .what do we. . .do?" Nigel managed, his face a ghostly pale. Bobby hoped the man didn't have a bad heart.

"Just do what they tell us to, all right? Most of the time they just want money and jewelry. Don't fight them—just give them what they want. Nothing is more important than your life," Bobby counseled in a calm voice. Inside, he was anything but calm. He was worried about his wife. While it was true that he didn't trust her or even desire to live with her, he didn't want anything to happen to her, either. Despite everything that had happened, he still loved her. That would take longer to die.

KIMBERLEY COMEAUX has been married twelve years to Brian, who is a music minister, a songwriter, and formally the lead singer for The Imperials. They have a son named Tyler, and the family currently resides in Louisiana. Kim turned her attention toward writing Christian fiction when she discovered songwriting wasn't for her, because she loves to read, especially romance. "I started out with an idea and before I knew it, I'd written a book-length story."

Books by Kimberley Comeaux

HEARTSONG PRESENTS
HP296—One More Chance
HP351—Courtin' Patience

Susannah's Secret

Kimberley Comeaux

Heartsong Presents

To my grandparents, S. R. and Levonne Nichols and Lonie Kennedy. Your family recollections and funny stories are my inspiration!

A note from the author:
I love to hear from my readers! You may correspond with me by writing: **Kimberley Comeaux**
Author Relations
PO Box 719
Uhrichsville, OH 44683

ISBN 1-58660-027-3

SUSANNAH'S SECRET

Cover illustration by Randy Hamblin.

PRINTED IN THE U.S.A.

prologue

Charleston, South Carolina—1887

Susannah Butler sat in her parents' parlor, in the plush blue-velvet chair, and listened with mounting trepidation as her father spoke. He'd lapsed into a familiar, long-winded speech about family and honor that she'd memorized long ago.

She tried to block out his words, to resist what he was saying; but as always, she could not. Guilt ate at her gut as he reminded her, yet again, that she was the only child he had left. The last Butler.

Except for one.

She couldn't believe he was going to force her to do it. Why couldn't he just let well enough alone? Her sister was dead, wasn't that enough?

But it wasn't enough. He wanted her sister's daughter, who lived with her daddy in Texas. He wanted to take little Beth away from the only home she'd ever known and bring her here, to the Butler mansion.

Beth would hate it here. Never mind the fact that she would be taken away from Bobby Joe Aaron, her father, and that she'd have to live with Susannah's overbearing father and ever-absent mother.

"Are you listening to me, Susannah?" her father growled as he stuck his beefy hands into the small pockets at his ample waist. He was a short, stocky man with fuzzy gray hair and matching bushy eyebrows that were always furled.

5

He was rarely seen without a cigar clamped between his teeth, and when he spoke, everyone within a hundred-yard radius could hear him. He liked it that way.

There was no one more important to Winston S. Butler than Winston himself.

Susannah cleared her throat and fiddled with the lacy handkerchief crumbled in her hand. "I'm listening, Daddy, but I don't see how I can do this. I don't even—"

"You're a Butler, girl," he interrupted with a scowl. "We don't know the meaning of the word *can't!* Now, are you going to complain some more or are you going to do what we've planned? You're our only hope here, Susannah. Don't let me down like. . ."

Susannah got up from her chair and planted her hands on her hips. "Like I did with Francis Bellington—is that what you were going to say, Daddy?"

"He is a millionaire three times over and would have made you a fine husband. He would have been a great addition to the Butler family."

Susannah had to laugh at that. "Daddy, I'm only twenty years old and he is seventy-five! The only great addition you wanted from the poor old man was his three million dollars! Now, I will do almost anything for you, but I have to draw a line sometimes, because—"

"Are you telling me that's what you're doing now? Are you drawing a line, Susannah?"

They stared at one another for a full minute.

A stranger walking into the room would not have been able to tell he was seeing father and daughter, for Susannah was so different from her father. Everyone said that she was the spitting image of her mother's mother. Tall, red wavy hair, a peachy complexion with only a few freckles splashed across her dainty nose, and brilliant green eyes—these all came together to make Susannah Butler one of the most beautiful women in Charleston.

But, boy, could she talk, which probably accounted for the fact that she was still single. It was known that she'd once been held up by a couple of robbers while riding on a stagecoach. She'd babbled on and on about how terrible it was for them to be doing what they were doing, which had distracted them so much that the sheriff was able to ride up and arrest them before they'd known what was happening.

"Daddy, do you think that Bobby Joe Aaron is going to just sit there and hand over his daughter to me? I can't think of a thing that would convince him to do such a thing, can you? I mean, let's look at this with a clear head! There are holes the size of. . .well, *Texas* in this plan! I think we need to sit down and—"

"How in the *world* am I supposed to look at anything with a clear head with all your yammering!" he said, putting his hands over his ears. He glared at her a moment, then dropped his hands. "Now then. If there are holes, then you're just going to have to think of some way to plug them up! I've tried to be reasonable about this by writing Aaron and asking him to let us see Elizabeth, but the man won't even dignify my request with a response!"

"But, Daddy, I don't think that gives us the right to—"

"That girl is a Butler and she belongs here. It's up to you to make it happen."

Her temper was starting to get the better of her. Susannah could feel the heat rising in her face. But like all true Southern women, she was prepared. Whipping out a silk fan from her skirt pocket, she began to fan herself rapidly. "May I also remind you, Daddy, that Beth is an Aaron, too? She belongs with her father."

"Her father," Winston spat out with distaste on his face, "is a no-account cowpoke!"

Susannah pursed her lips as she continued to fan, harder now. "He's not a 'cowpoke'; he owns a sawmill!"

Winston yanked the cigar stub out of his mouth and ground it into the ashtray on a small end table. "He's a Texan. What's the difference?"

Susannah stopped fanning and frowned. "You don't know the dif—"

"Of course I know the difference! I was just making a point!"

Susannah rolled her eyes. "I think you could have come up with a different way to make that point. I mean, if you'd said—"

"Are you going to stand there and talk me to death, or are you going to go to Texas?"

Say no! her mind screamed at her. But she just couldn't do it. She was his only child and he depended on her—even if his thinking was crazy, not to mention self-centered.

"Oh, all right," she conceded with a sigh. "But don't blame me if I can't do it. I'll try. That's all I can do." She opened and closed her fan while she thought a moment about what she wanted to say.

Finally, with chin raised, she spoke. "And while I'm over there in Texas dillydallying in my poor brother-in-law's business, I'm also going to be praying." She raised her hand to stop the argument that she knew would come. "Now, I know you aren't a religious man, Daddy. I'm just warning you that if I feel that God is telling me to forget the whole business and come back to South Carolina, that's what I'm going to do!"

He opened his mouth again, but she pressed on. "And if I feel that it's in the best interest of Beth to bring her back here, then so be it. But, I'm telling you right now, Daddy, I'm going to be on my knees every morning and night. And what I'll be praying for most of all is that God will talk to that cold heart of yours and make you come to your senses!"

"You never mind about my senses! Just bring the child back!"

She shook her head with pity as her father turned to pull another cigar out of the fancy case on the fireplace mantle. She prayed every night that her father would come to accept Christ in his heart, like she had. She was the only one in the family who was a believer, now that her sister was gone. It had been the girls' governess, Mrs. Oglethorp, who had led Susannah to the Lord. Of course, when her father discovered that she was teaching them from the Bible, Mrs. Oglethorp had been promptly dismissed.

In Winston Butler's mind, religion of any kind was for the weak. It had no place in the Butler household.

Susannah started to leave, but something still nagged at her. "Daddy? Just what am I supposed to do when I get to Springton, Texas? How am I supposed to explain my presence there?"

Her father nonchalantly lit a cigar. "I've managed to get you a job as the town's schoolteacher. You start as soon as you get there."

Susannah stood in stunned silence for a moment. All her life she'd dreamed about becoming a teacher, and although she'd had plenty of schooling, her father would never permit her to work. Now, here he was, handing her dream to her on a silver platter.

A dream with conditions.

"I'll give you a year to figure out some way to get Elizabeth and bring her back. After that, if you're not successful, I'll do the job, my way. But regardless, you'll be coming home," he informed her in no uncertain terms.

Finding it difficult to contain her excitement, she nodded and flew out of the parlor. It didn't matter if it was only for a year. She was going to savor and enjoy this year so that she would have it to look back on in later years.

As she ran up the wide marble staircase, she whispered a prayer of thanks to God for giving her this opportunity. He'd always taken such good care of her in the past, helping her through the difficult days after she'd lost her sister, and now He was blessing her beyond anything she could have imagined.

She was going to be a teacher!

Springton, Texas, might be just a cowpoke town to her daddy, but suddenly it had become paradise to Susannah!

❧

Springton, Texas—one month later

"Brother Caleb!" Bobby Joe Aaron called out to Springton's minister, who had been busy fixing a loose board on his front porch. Caleb looked up and waved as Bobby Joe opened the white gate to the reverend's yard. "I'm sorry I missed the town meeting. Was anything decided about a schoolteacher?"

Caleb put down his hammer and stood up. "Hello, Bobby Joe." He shook hands with the tall man as he nodded his head. "Lucky for us, we got a qualified applicant's résumé in yesterday's mail, just in time for the meeting. She's from back east, she's single, and she has been to some mighty impressive schools. She was more qualified than the rest, so we decided to hire her."

Bobby Joe nodded his head. "That's great. I had hired a tutor for Beth, but I'd rather that she was around other kids."

What Beth really needed was a mother, but he didn't say that to the preacher. The more his daughter was around all his brothers and himself, the more tomboyish she became. She needed a mother to show her how to be a little lady. The only problem with that was, he would have to marry to get her one! Bobby wasn't sure he was ready for another marriage. Not if it ended like his last one had.

Brother Caleb nodded and looked at Bobby Joe with interest. "So how are you these days, Bobby Joe? I'm still looking for you on Sundays, you know."

Bobby Joe smiled, but it held a trace of bitterness. "I just don't feel up for church these days, Reverend."

"I know that, and part of me understands. But God is right there to help you if you need Him. Day or night. All you have to do is ask."

Bobby Joe nodded as he shuffled his boot about on the porch step, clearly uncomfortable. "Well, I just wondered about the meeting. I'll let you get back to your work." He started to turn away, then remembered to ask, "By the way, what is her name?"

Caleb frowned, not understanding, then suddenly his face cleared. "Oh, you mean the teacher! Last name is Butler. . . Susannah Butler, I believe. She's coming from South Carolina."

Every last bit of color left Bobby Joe's face. Surely this couldn't be his wife's sister! He swallowed. "That wouldn't be. . .Charleston, South Carolina, would it?" he asked slowly.

Caleb nodded as he reached for his hammer again, missing the shocked expression on Bobby Joe's face. "Yeah, I believe that's it!"

Bobby Joe took a deep breath, then straightened his hat. "Maybe I'll keep that tutor on for a few more years," he mumbled as he turned away.

"What was that?" Brother Caleb called after him.

"I said, see ya later, Reverend," he lied as he walked out of the yard.

He had tried so desperately to forget Leanna, the woman who had walked out on him, leaving him and their daughter alone. She'd broken his heart and made him lose faith in everything and everyone.

Left him feeling so alone.

Everyone had told him that her dying just weeks after she'd left was a result of her sins, that God had punished her for what she'd done and had taken her life.

And that was the biggest reason he was angry now. God had taken her away before he had a chance to get her back.

Now her sister was coming.

The way Bobby Joe figured it, the Butlers were the reason that she had left in the first place. They never thought he was good enough, and Winston Butler never missed an opportunity to let him know it.

Leanna must have left because the old man had gotten to her at last.

He didn't want anything to do with the Butlers. And while he didn't know why Susannah wanted to live in the same town as he did, he was going to stay out of her way.

Forgetting. . .was going to be a lot harder now.

one

Ten months later

The warm sun shone bright upon the little town of Springton, Texas, and although everybody was complaining about how hot it was, Susannah Butler loved every degree of heat. In fact, there wasn't much she didn't like about the little town. She loved her teaching job and the kids that filled her days with fun and learning. She loved her friends—Rachel and Patience and all the other folks she'd met in her brief stay. She loved her niece, although she didn't get to see her that much. And she loved the little blue house that went with the teaching position.

Springton, Texas, was a far cry from Charleston, and Susannah liked it that way. The town consisted of just one long street with a mercantile; a blacksmith's shop; a sheriff's office, where her friend Lee Cutler held the office of sheriff; the bank; the Springton Inn; the Golden Lady Saloon (a place that the women of Springton were praying would close down); the First Church of Springton with its orphanage; and the parsonage, where her friends Rev. Caleb and Rachel Stone lived. At the end of the street was the schoolhouse, her little blue house situated just behind it. The house was located near the creek that bordered the town.

It was such a lovely place to live, and despite her father's pleading and threats, Susannah was determined to live here for a long time!

Oh, she worried from time to time what her father would do at the end of the planned year. But she knew she would have no part of his scheme to take Beth away from her father, Bobby Joe Aaron.

Which brought her to the one thing that did bother her. . . .

While Susannah loved just about everything and everybody in her new Texas town. . .it seemed that not everybody loved her!

Bobby Joe Aaron was the most hardheaded, infuriating, judgmental man she'd ever had the misfortune of meeting. Ever since she'd stepped foot in the town, he'd done his level best to make her feel like an outcast. He wouldn't talk to her, would barely even look at her; and what aggravated Susannah the most was that he wouldn't let her see her niece, Beth.

Why? That question had plagued her for ten long months, and she didn't have an answer. She knew that her sister's death had hurt him badly; however, Susannah didn't understand why he seemed to blame her for it.

But Susannah had a secret. A secret that she swore to her sister she wouldn't tell—and she hadn't told a soul in years. Well, that promise was made to a dying woman who probably hadn't been able to think clearly because of the tumor in her brain. It was a promise that she could no longer keep from Bobby Joe Aaron.

Susannah took a deep breath as she straightened the little hat perched upon her carefully arranged hairdo and smoothed back a few stray tresses that had come loose on her ride out to the Aaron homestead. She would not think about her feelings about Bobby Joe Aaron and the way it pained her that he seemed to want nothing to do with her. Instead she would concentrate on why she'd ridden out to meet with him.

Today. . .she had come to tell him the truth.

She took another look at the huge brick house with its six white columns and then started to climb from the wagon. As she stepped down, she began to pray aloud. "Oh, Lord. . . please give me the words to say. I know that sounds like a strange request coming from a jabbermouth like me, because You of all people know I can talk 'til the cows come home, but I really do need Your help today. You see, if I can just find out why—"

"Who are you talking to?"

At the sound of the deep voice that she recognized right away, she whirled around and smiled sheepishly. "I was. . . uh. . .praying. I mean, He's everywhere, isn't He! You can talk to Him while you're walking down the road or weeding your garden. . .or. . .even milking a cow. I'll bet. . ." Her nervous, high-pitched voice faded away when he remained unsmiling, even glowering at her.

She tugged at her gloves and with false bravado tilted her chin forward. "I'll bet you're wanting to know what I'm doing here."

Bobby Joe folded his arms, and his lips thinned grimly. "For starters."

Staring at all six feet, four inches of the dark-headed man almost made her lose her nerve. With his ice-blue eyes and tanned skin, he was an extremely handsome man who had made her heart go all aflutter on a number of occasions. But he had a way of scowling at her that quickly brought her back to reality. She understood why her sister had been so attracted to him, but he must have been a lot more mannerly and cordial when Leanna had met him; otherwise, she'd never have married him. Susannah didn't see any evidence of that old Bobby Joe now.

And it was too bad that man no longer existed; he might

have liked her as much as she liked him.

"I think we need to talk," she said quickly.

He just stared at her.

She swallowed and tried again. "I need to talk to you about Leanna."

His piercing gaze seemed to bore a hole through her. "Why?"

Susannah took a breath to calm her jumping nerves. She really wished he would be more open and friendly. "You need to know the truth about why she left to go home to Charleston."

His eyes turned fiery, his countenance no longer grim but angry. He took a step closer to her, causing her to back up against the wagon in fear. "What kind of game are you and your father playing now? I've never figured out why you came to Springton—how you could possibly leave your cushy lifestyle and live in a tiny house in a town I've heard your father call 'uncivilized.' If you thought you could come to stir up trouble and cause me or my family any more hurt, you've got another think coming."

He jammed the hat he'd been holding on his head and gave her a look of disgust. But Susannah was quick to notice a touch of pain in his eyes. "Now, I want you to get back in your wagon and get off my property. You're trespassing." With those heated words, he turned and started back to the house.

Susannah's mind whirled as she stared after him, trying to make sense of what he'd just said. She never dreamed he wouldn't want to hear her. For some silly reason she thought he would want to know about her sister's mysterious departure.

"Wait!" she called after him, just as the door shut soundly behind him. Undaunted, Susannah ran up to the door and was surprised to find it unlocked. Boldly she opened the door and entered.

Bobby Joe turned just as she walked onto the marble floor, and she skidded to a halt. She noticed that he'd tossed his hat on the table beside the door. "I don't think you heard me. . . ," he began, when she interrupted him.

"Oh, I heard, all right. But you are not the only one involved here. I've carried this secret around for four years now, and I don't want to lug it around one more minute! I don't know why Leanna didn't tell you the truth, but it's not what you think."

Pain rippled across his strong features, and she could tell he was struggling to control his emotions. "What could you possibly tell me to make this better, Susannah? What secret could make this all go away? Why would my wife leave her husband who loved her and her young daughter who needed her?"

Susannah shook her head. "She had her reasons. . . ."

"You know, she was happy until you both started sending her letters. I don't know what you said to her, but it was enough to make her draw away from Beth and me. Within weeks she became withdrawn and irritable with both of us. Before I knew what was happening, she was gone." He turned away and paced to the large staircase in the foyer, then sat down on the bottom step. Rubbing a hand down his face, he continued. "I was frantic. I thought she'd been kidnapped or had hurt herself and was unable to reach the house."

Susannah could do nothing but stand there and blink back tears. Her sister had caused this man more pain by withholding the truth about her illness than she would have by telling him in the first place. *Why, Leanna?*

"Then I found the telegraph from your father. It said that you and he would be waiting for her at the train station in Charleston." He looked up at her with haunted eyes. Eyes full of sadness and bitterness. "What did you say to her to make her start hating me? What was so wrong with her being married to me and living a decent life here in Springton?"

Tears spilled from Susannah's eyes as she stared at him. "Oh, Bobby Joe, it wasn't like that. . . ." She put her shaking hand over her mouth as she tried to keep herself from crying. "You see, she—"

Bobby Joe abruptly stood up. "You know what? I don't want to hear it." His face was angry again as he came closer to her. "Don't you understand that it's not going to make a difference? Why are you doing this, anyway? Is it guilt that brought you here? Are you trying to make amends for the part you played in all this?"

"That's not it. . .I—"

He pointed his finger in her face. "You can't possibly tell me anything that is going to make this any better. I'm sorry you're feeling bad, but I feel worse. Now I want you to leave."

"I can't leave until you know the truth!"

He backed away and threw his arms up. "Okay, you win. Tell me the truth, Susannah. Tell me the truth that's going to make this ordeal better."

Susannah looked down. "Nothing will make it better, but I can help you to understand." She looked back up at him and met his blue eyes with her own light green ones. "Leanna was dying of a brain tumor. She was on her way to Charleston to get medical treatment, not to leave you. She made me promise not to tell you until she knew the doctors could cure her. She died before she arrived in Charleston. I tried to contact you. . . ."

For what seemed like an hour, he just stared at her in horror, as his eyes grew damp. Slowly he turned from her, walked back to the staircase, and leaned upon the massive railing with his head bent low.

"Why didn't you tell me this sooner?" he asked in a low, hoarse voice.

Susannah wiped a tear from her face. "I told you, she made me promise not to."

He kept his back to her. "Then why now?"

"I realized that I made the promise to a dying woman who probably wasn't thinking clearly. I have seen how badly you've been hurt, and I thought you deserved to hear the truth."

He was quiet for a moment, and then he spoke. "I deserved to know the truth four years ago." With that, he walked around the banister and into a room farther down the hall, closing the door soundly behind him.

A huge ache squeezed at her heart as she watched him leave the room. She had the most incredible urge to run after him and wrap her arms around him in comfort. She had known for a few months that she had growing feelings for Bobby Joe. She just didn't understand them—wasn't sure that she wanted to.

Now what? she thought. Wrapping her arms about herself, she looked around the beautiful grand foyer and wondered what the future would bring. Would he understand why she had kept her secret from him? Would he even believe her?

Those questions hung in the air around her like a heavy weight as she turned and left the house.

On the way back to town, Susannah prayed. Prayed for him, prayed for herself, and prayed that God would somehow work a miracle.

≈

Bobby Joe paced the carpeted floor of his library as he thought about what Susannah had just told him. It couldn't be true. Leanna couldn't have been sick—she would have told him. . .wouldn't she? Why would she keep something like this from him?

His memory whirled back to a time before she left. Several times he'd caught her crying. Each time, when he had questioned her or showed concern, she had turned away and shut him out. For two months she had slowly pulled away from Beth and him. He'd thought it was because of the letters and telegrams she'd been getting from her father and sister. He'd blamed them for his wife's coldness and for her deserting them.

At that time he'd thought that his wife had stopped loving him, that she'd become tired of being a wife and mother. He'd thought there must have been something lacking within him; maybe his love hadn't been enough.

Then for weeks he had prayed that God would help their relationship, that He would work a miracle and make her start loving him again. . . . But there was no miracle. And when she left him, he'd stopped praying. . .and he stopped believing in God.

At least he tried. When the new preacher, Brother Caleb, arrived in Springton, he had befriended Bobby Joe, and he never ceased in his effort to let Bobby Joe know that God loved him. Bobby Joe had been shown such love and kindness by the preacher and his wife that he'd relented and had allowed his daughter to attend Sunday school. But he himself hadn't made that step to make things right with God. He didn't know if he ever could.

And if this news were true, why hadn't God allowed him to see the truth? Why had He allowed Bobby Joe to suffer through an illusion?

There were too many whys and too few answers.

At that moment his seven-year-old daughter came skipping into the room, giving him a brief respite from his troubled thoughts.

"Hi, Daddy! Whatcha doing?" she asked as she plopped herself on top of his huge oak desk.

"I was just thinkin' about something, sweetheart," he told her as he walked over and sat down beside her. Ruffling her long brown curls, his gaze ran lovingly over her dainty features, marveling at how much she looked like his mother. She had some of Leanna about her, too, but the blue eyes and upturned nose were from his side of the family.

"Are you thinking about Aunt Susannah? I saw her ride off in her buggy when I looked out my window a little while ago," she mentioned innocently.

Bobby Joe sighed. "I guess so, Beth. . . . Uh. . .you didn't happen to hear what we were talking about when she was here, did you?"

Beth picked up a glass paperweight from his desk and turned it around in her small hands. "No. I was too busy drawing a new picture."

"Beth," he said in a scolding voice. "Aren't you supposed to be studying? Where is Mr. Copeland, anyway?" he asked, referring to the wiry, balding man he'd hired as her tutor.

She shrugged. "He drank some of his medicine, and then he went to sleep as I was doing my arithmetic. I didn't know what else to do, so I've been drawing."

Bobby Joe frowned. "Medicine?"

"Yes, sir. He keeps his medicine in a little silver bottle tucked inside his coat."

"And just how often does Mr. Copeland take this. . .this 'medicine'?" he asked, trying to remain calm. His temper, however, was rising with every passing second.

"Oh, all the time! He must be sick a lot." Beth scooted off the desk and put down the paperweight. "Can I go outside and swing?"

Bobby Joe stood with her. "That's a good idea. Just stay in the yard and—"

"Don't talk to the workers. I know, Daddy!" she finished for him with a roll of her eyes. He told her repeatedly to stay away from the workers at the sawmill adjacent to the house. Most were good men, but he didn't trust all of them.

As she ran out of the room, he made his way up the staircase to the drunken teacher he'd hired for his beloved daughter. He would have to fire him and find another tutor.

You could just send her to the school and let Susannah teach her, a little voice nagged in his head. And for the first time, he contemplated it. But he didn't know what to think about Susannah anymore. He didn't know what to think about what she'd told him.

For the first time in a long while, Bobby Joe—the head of his family since he was seventeen and the man who ran the family sawmill and made all the decisions—didn't know what to do next. Never had he felt more confused and less in control of his life.

Never had he felt so alone.

He was going to have to deal with Susannah and what she'd told him, though. And he had to do it soon.

two

For the rest of the day Susannah had held out a small hope that Bobby Joe would come by her house so that they could come to some sort of understanding. Every time she heard a wagon, she would run to the window, only to be disappointed when it wasn't him.

Why she thought Bobby Joe would want to have anything to do with her after she had kept such an important secret from him, she didn't know. A silly hope that he would want to forgive her? Yes. An even sillier hope that he would start to like her? Susannah wouldn't even allow herself to answer that!

So she waited all day and evening, but to no avail. Bobby Joe didn't come, and she realized that he probably never would. It was too late. There was too much hurt and bitterness.

The next day was Sunday, and Susannah was so depressed that she contemplated staying home. But what would that accomplish? She'd just end up feeling more sorry for herself. And besides, God shouldn't be neglected just because she was feeling down.

Singing and preaching were just what she needed to lift her spirits. So, dressed in her nicest blue dress with its eyelet lace accents, she walked, Bible in hand, to the little church down the lane.

When she arrived, she sat in her usual seat in the third row next to Patience and Lee Cutler.

"Good morning, Susannah!" Patience greeted. She was

wearing a flattering peach dress that had been designed and sewn by Rachel, the Reverend Caleb Stone's wife. But while the dress always seemed to complement Patience's pale skin, today she looked even more radiant and glowing. "I have something to tell you!"

Susannah smiled as she looked over at Lee's beaming smile and then turned back to Patience, as Patience placed a hand over her stomach. She gasped, "You're going to have a baby, aren't you?"

"Yes!" Patience answered in a hushed giggle as the two young women hugged. "Doc Benson confirmed it yesterday. I had a feeling that I was, but I wasn't sure until I talked to him."

"You thought you were with child and you didn't tell me?" Susannah scolded with mock indignation.

"Well, I was afraid to tell anyone about it. . .just in case it wasn't true."

Lee leaned over to join the conversation. "She didn't even tell me until yesterday!"

Susannah smiled at him. "Congratulations, Sheriff. You two will be the greatest parents in all of Texas!"

Lee had once courted Susannah for a few weeks, before they'd both realized he had feelings for Patience. But Susannah hadn't minded. She hadn't had feelings for him, either. Her mind at the time had been so much on Beth and on her own rocky relationship with Bobby Joe.

Susannah was glad that Lee and Patience were able to realize their love for one another. Their courtship and marriage had been like what Susannah dreamed she would have someday, once she met the right man.

Patience smiled at her husband, then turned toward Susannah. "I am nervous and excited all at the same time, and. . ." Her words trailed off as her eyes left Susannah and focused on something behind her. "Oh, my! If I wasn't seeing it, I wouldn't believe it!"

Susannah turned her head, curious at Patience's sudden change of subject, and froze.

Patience had been right. It was unbelievable!

"Bobby Joe Aaron hasn't been to church in two years!" Patience said in a hushed, excited voice. Then she called out, "Hi, Bobby Joe! Why don't you come sit with us?"

Susannah gave a quick intake of breath as she looked pointedly at Patience. "Don't do that! He won't come, and I'll be plum embarrassed!"

"Oh, don't be a silly-willy, as you would say! He's coming this way!" she whispered. "Uh, Susannah, aren't you going to scoot over and let Bobby Joe sit down?" she said louder.

After sending her friend a glare, Susannah made herself look up at Bobby Joe. She almost cringed when she saw him intently staring at her. "Uh, sure," she said sheepishly as she scooted over. "Have a seat, Bobby."

Bobby Joe sat down and leaned close to her. He was clean shaven and his dark brown hair was still slightly damp. He smelled of soap and clean summer air, and Susannah was sure that she'd smelled nothing nicer. She also noticed the sharply pressed black suit that he wore, along with a crisp white shirt and ribbon tie. He was such a handsome man, but Susannah was trying hard not to notice that.

"Can we talk after the service?" he asked in a low voice.

Chills rose on her bare arms as his breath caressed her ear. She swallowed hard, trying to relieve the sudden dryness in her throat. "Oh. . .okay," she stammered, wishing she hadn't sounded as if she'd been caught off guard.

"What did he say?" Patience whispered in her other ear.

Susannah leaned over with her hand cupped over her mouth. "I'll tell you later."

"Why can't you tell me now?"

Susannah looked with exasperation at her nosy friend. "Because!" Her mouth had formed the word without sound.

"Is Bobby Joe courting you?" she whispered louder than Susannah would have liked. "Oh, my goodness, Susannah! Why didn't you tell me?"

Susannah was frantically shaking her head. "That's not it, Patience. He—"

"You and Bobby Joe are courting?" Lee asked in a normal voice, loud enough that the people in the pews in front of them could hear. And of course, Bobby Joe heard, too.

Susannah turned the color of her hair, and she closed her eyes for a moment, wishing she could disappear. When she opened them, there were about ten pairs of eyes staring at her and Bobby Joe with nosy interest.

She didn't even look Bobby Joe's way. She didn't have enough courage.

Turning fully to face Patience and Lee, she said very clearly, "We are not cour—"

But she didn't get to finish her sentence.

"Good morning, everyone. So good to see you all here," Brother Caleb said from the pulpit. And then the service began.

Susannah slowly faced forward, humiliated beyond belief and wishing that this was a dream. Like all small towns, people here liked to gossip, especially about who was courting whom. A rumor would be all over town by afternoon, headed toward the next county.

And what was Bobby Joe thinking? He never came to church, and she was so afraid that this was going to keep him from ever coming again.

The organ began to play and everyone stood up, opening their hymnals to the first song, "Christ the Lord Is Risen Today." Susannah was surprised when she heard Bobby Joe's baritone voice join in with the others.

After a moment, she gathered enough courage to take a quick peek up at him. To her surprise, he glanced down at her at the same time, and he was actually grinning!

He shook his head and looked at her as one would an amusing child, then looked back to the song leader. He actually thought this was funny!

She looked over at Patience and noticed that she wasn't even pretending to sing. She was looking back and forth at Bobby Joe and Susannah with great interest, smiling knowingly.

Susannah felt compelled to give her a nudge. "Would you stop?"

Patience opened her hymnal, but then whispered to Susannah, "I knew it!"

"Knew what?"

"I'll tell you later," she teased, repeating Susannah's own words.

Susannah looked back down at her open hymnal and sighed.

☙

After church, and after avoiding inquiring stares, Susannah and Bobby Joe made their way to the Springton Inn, where a small restaurant was located. When they were shown to their table, Bobby Joe gallantly held out Susannah's chair for her, then sat down across from her.

They were both noticeably uncomfortable. Susannah spoke first. "I'd like to apologize about the misunderstanding with Patience in the church. I don't know why she came to the conclusion that we were. . .well. . .that we were. . ."

Bobby raised an eyebrow as he looked at her. "Courting?" he supplied calmly. He didn't seem upset about it, but with Bobby Joe you really couldn't tell. He was not one to show his emotions openly.

"Uh. . .yes. That was an unfortunate little episode, wasn't it?" Out came her fan, and she rapidly began fanning her reddening face.

"Well, don't expect that to be the last we'll hear of it. If I know Springton folk, it's probably spread to Dallas by now," he drawled, watching the movement of her fan. If she didn't know better, she'd think he was amused!

Susannah stopped fanning and frowned at him. "But it's not true!"

Bobby Joe just shrugged and looked down at the handwritten menu.

Susannah sighed and looked at her own menu. She sneaked a couple of peaks at Bobby Joe and was embarrassed when he caught her the second time. Quickly she lowered her eyes. If only she could tell what he was thinking! The man had a poker face if she ever saw one.

One thing was for sure, though; he didn't seem to hate her anymore. Before, he wouldn't even look at her. Now, here he was, acting like a gentleman.

Susannah prayed that they could work things out. And even as she prayed, another thought nagged at her. She needed to tell him about her father's plans! Her year was almost up, and Susannah knew that if she didn't do what her father wanted, he would probably come and try to take Beth himself. And he would probably be armed with a passel of lawyers to see the deed done. Winston Butler would use any means he could to win—of that Susannah had no doubt.

But she wouldn't tell him, not just yet. He might be beginning to actually like her. She didn't want to change that by bringing up her father's ugly plan.

So she smiled brightly at him and asked, "So where's Beth today?"

Bobby Joe lowered his menu. "I left her with Daniel. I thought we could talk better if she weren't here."

"Oh," was all she could think of saying. So he wanted to talk. *Is that good?* she wondered.

"I've thought about what you told me, and I would—"

The innkeeper interrupted him as he brought over two glasses of iced tea.

After the innkeeper took their order, Bobby Joe continued. "As I was saying, I would like you to tell me all you know about what happened with Leanna. I still can't understand why she wouldn't tell me."

"All I can come up with is that the tumor affected her thinking and reasoning. She knew that the doctor in Tyler couldn't help her, so she wrote home to Father. She thought that with her occasional blackouts, she might hurt Beth. And she wrote that she didn't want to worry you, that she would tell you what she was doing once she got to Charleston. But—"

"But she never made it," Bobby Joe finished for her.

"No, she didn't, and I'm so sorry we didn't tell you sooner, Bobby Joe. I just. . ." Her voice drifted off, unable to find the right words. With a sigh, she shook her head sadly. "Will we ever get past this, Bobby? Can you ever forgive me?"

He stared at her intently for a moment. Susannah could only guess what was going through his mind. However, she thought she knew his answer. After all, he had gotten used to ignoring her and shutting her out of his life.

But he surprised her.

"I think I should be asking that question. If anyone owes an apology, it's me. I guess I wanted someone to blame, and since Leanna was going to Charleston when she died, I thought you'd convinced her to leave me." He sighed and ran a hand through his dark hair.

He looked so sad and lost sitting there, and Susannah's heart went out to him. Nothing could be done to erase the years that he had lived in bitterness and hatred toward her and her father. There was only the future, and only God could help them with that. And it was the future that she was most interested in.

"Leanna was the happiest I'd ever seen her the day she married you, Bobby. I don't believe we could have said anything to convince her to leave you. She wrote to me constantly, going on and on about how wonderful her life was with you and Beth."

Susannah could have sworn that his eyes became red and watery, but he blinked and the redness was gone. On impulse, Susannah reached out and put her hand over his. Surprisingly, Bobby Joe turned his hand over and held hers firmly. "Thank you for telling me that," he said in a gruff voice. He then let go of her hand and leaned back in his chair. Brushing a hand down his face in a weary gesture, he admitted, "I don't know what to do now. I've spent all this time playing the jilted husband and lashing out at just about everyone. . .even God." His voice drifted off with a sigh. "I just don't know."

"Bobby, you need time, that's all."

He nodded. "I know." He paused a minute and then looked back at her. "You know, you are the only one besides my mother who has ever called me Bobby."

Susannah smiled, knowing that he needed to change the

subject and lighten the mood. "I'm sorry. It just seems to fit you better than tagging on Joe at the end."

He shrugged. "I don't mind it."

They talked a few minutes more, and then their food arrived, putting a lull in their conversation.

When they had finished and Bobby Joe had paid the bill, he escorted her toward his buggy, which was still tied up at the church.

For most of their lunch Susannah had been trying to figure out how to broach the subject of Beth, and when they'd almost reached the church, she decided to just go ahead and tell him what was on her mind. "Bobby, is there any chance you'd let Beth come and visit me soon? I know I may be asking too much, but I really love her, and—"

Bobby put out his hand to stop her. "That's just one more thing I'm going to have to apologize for, I guess. You can see Beth any time you want. In fact, I just fired her tutor, and I think it would be good for her to attend your school."

A smile spread over Susannah's face, and her heart suddenly felt light and carefree. It seemed as though a miracle had taken place. Just days ago, Bobby Joe would not even have said hello. Now here he was, being open and friendly.

"Oh, Bobby! That's wonderful! I know that she'll love being with the other kids," she exclaimed cheerfully, her Southern drawl becoming more pronounced. "I just don't know how much more good news I can take!"

Bobby Joe smiled one of his rare smiles, although it was a small one, and motioned toward his wagon. "Can I drive you home?"

Susannah was tempted, but it would be silly to allow him to do so. She lived so close to the church. Besides, she needed time to sort through her feelings and come to grips with this new friendship she and Bobby Joe seemed to be forming.

"No, thank you. It's such a pretty day, I think I'll walk," she replied.

Bobby Joe nodded and tipped his Stetson to her. "I'll be in contact with you about school."

Susannah nodded and watched him climb up into his wagon. As he drove away, she admired his dark, wavy hair that brushed his collar and his broad, muscular shoulders and arms as they handled the wagon.

She was in big trouble with a capital T! She had been attracted to Bobby Joe ever since she had stepped off the train at Springton. And that was when he had been grouchy and hateful to her. Now, with him being nice and smiling at her, she liked him more than ever.

But Susannah knew that a cauldron was brewing. She may have stopped him from hating her by divulging one secret, but what would he do when he found out the other one? How would he respond once he found out why she had come to Springton? Would he turn away from her again? Probably.

Susannah whispered a prayer to God, asking that He'd help her explain the secret. She would need a perfect time and place to tell Bobby Joe. And she would need courage. . . courage to tell a man that she'd been sent to Springton to take his daughter from him.

three

Bobby Joe wasn't surprised to find all three of his brothers waiting for him at the front door of their home. The Aaron brothers were all large men, like their big brother, and they had similar features. But their hair was another matter. While Billy Ray had lighter brown hair than Bobby Joe, Tommy's hair was so blond it was almost white, and Daniel's hair was a deep auburn. All three of them were staring at him, with arms folded and eyes narrowed.

"So what's this we hear about you courting Susannah Butler?" Billy Ray asked first.

"Yeah! We didn't think you even liked her!" Daniel accused.

"What I can't figure out is when you've had time to court anyone! You're either in the house or at the mill, unless. . ." Tommy's eyes widened as he was struck with a thought. "You haven't been sneaking out at night, have you?"

Bobby Joe had figured this would happen. He hadn't been exaggerating when he'd told Susannah that this would be all over town within minutes.

Sighing, he pulled off his hat and slapped it against his pants leg. "No, Billy, I'm not courting Susannah. But I do not dislike her, Daniel. And for your information, Tommy, if I decided to court a woman, you can bet your boots I wouldn't resort to sneaking out at midnight to do it!"

The brothers looked at each other with sheepish faces and then turned back to their eldest sibling. "Well, how were we supposed to know? Zeke made a special trip out here to tell us about it. Says it's big news around town," Billy Ray defended.

Bobby Joe rested his hands on his hips. "Zeke wasn't even in church."

Daniel shrugged. "He heard it from Nancy Will's brother."

"Now there's a reliable source," Bobby Joe said dryly as he pushed past them and entered the house.

"Aw, come on, Bobby Joe. Where are they getting it, then? What's up with you and the schoolteacher?" Daniel persisted.

Bobby Joe sighed and turned to them with a serious expression on his face. "Before we get into that subject, I need to ask you boys a question about Leanna."

All three of them looked at Bobby Joe with more than a little surprise, and for a moment, no one spoke.

Finally, Billy Ray broke the shocked silence. "Bobby Joe, I thought we were never to mention her name," he said hesitantly.

Bobby Joe ignored him and continued. "Did any of you see Leanna display strange behavior before she left?"

Tommy and Daniel, both Billy Ray's elders, shrugged their shoulders. "We weren't in the house that much, big brother," Tommy told him. "If she had been acting funny, I didn't even notice."

Bobby Joe nodded with a deflated sigh. He started to tell them what happened with Susannah, when Billy Ray spoke up.

"I noticed, Bobby Joe. She cried a lot and seemed to be troubled. She didn't know that I knew, but I would see her when I came home from school." He had only been fifteen when she left.

Bobby Joe's insides twisted at the thought of his late wife suffering alone. He wondered again why she kept everything to herself—why she wouldn't let him help her through that scary time.

He took a breath, then he revealed to his brothers everything that Susannah had told him.

Billy Ray blew out a big breath of air. "So that means Susannah and her father had nothing to do with Leanna's leaving!"

Daniel smiled at his brother innocently. "Yeah, that means you can court her if you want to."

Bobby Joe ignored his brother and addressed Billy Ray's comment. "That's right, Billy. That's why I went to church this morning. I wanted to meet up with her to apologize."

Tommy looked at Daniel and nudged him. "Has Bobby Joe ever apologized to *us* for anything?"

"Naw, he only apologizes to the women he's sweet on," Daniel drawled.

After fixing them with a narrowed look, Bobby Joe moved past them, and, tossing his hat on the rack beside the door, he made his way back to the kitchen, where he knew his daughter would be. She liked to sit and talk with their cook and housekeeper, Lucy Martin.

Just before he made it to the kitchen door, he stopped and turned back to his brothers when Daniel, in his usual kidding manner, made a flippant statement.

"Since the whole town thinks you're courting one another, why don't you just go ahead and do it?" He laughed as he winked at Tommy and Billy. "She's already practically family, being Leanna's sister and all."

A shocked quiet settled quickly over the group as the words slipped out of Daniel's mouth. It was a stupid thing to say, and the brothers all knew it. Tommy and Billy glared at Daniel, who flushed guiltily as he looked at his eldest brother, preparing to apologize.

But the words never made it out of his mouth.

Bobby Joe wasn't angry; he wasn't even irritated. It was like a seed had been planted in his brain and refused to go away! And because this showed on his face with the lift of a thoughtful brow, his brothers could do nothing but stare.

Thanks to Daniel, an idea was taking shape in his mind, and it seemed to be the answer to all his problems. Susannah *was* practically family, and she did seem to love his daughter. And despite his efforts to keep them apart, Beth liked her aunt, too.

But Bobby Joe wasn't considering courting Susannah, he was thinking about striking up a deal with her—a deal that would give his daughter the mother she needed and his home a much-needed female influence.

Marrying Susannah made sense. Not for romantic reasons or any such nonsense. He'd already been through that and didn't want to suffer from love again. No. A marriage of convenience would suit him better.

The more he thought about it, the more he liked the idea. He smiled a satisfied smile as he looked up at his brothers.

They were staring at him like he'd just grown a couple of horns.

"What?" he asked innocently.

"You ain't really thinking of. . ." Tommy drifted off, the words seeming too ludicrous to utter.

"You know, I believe he is," Daniel commented incredulously. "I was only kidding, big brother."

"Y'all are crazy," Billy Ray scoffed. But upon looking at Bobby Joe more closely, he became less sure. "Uh. . .they are crazy, aren't they, Bobby Joe?"

But Bobby Joe was never much of a talker. He just

shrugged his shoulders and walked into the kitchen, leaving his brothers with confusion written all over their faces.

ಬಾ

Susannah's short walk home turned out to be the longest she'd traveled in a while! Everyone in Springton seemed to have chosen to be in town that afternoon, just so they could talk to her—at least that's how it appeared.

Oh, they were clever about it. First they would ask her how she'd been, then they'd slowly turn the conversation to having seen her either sitting with Bobby Joe in church or at the restaurant. Susannah kept telling them that it was nothing, that Bobby Joe was just her brother-in-law, nothing more.

Not a soul believed her.

She'd gotten so tired of being stopped and plied with polite conversation (which was, in fact, just a cover for nosing around in her business), that she practically screamed at one man.

He came up to her and began, "Pardon me, but—"

"Look, mister!" she interrupted. "Bobby Joe is just my brother-in-law, okay? You really shouldn't listen to gossip!"

The man blinked and took a step back. "I. . .I was only going to ask you where the stables are located," he stammered, causing Susannah to blush with embarrassment.

She hurried on down the street, but everywhere she looked, groups of women, young and old, were standing around talking, whispering, and giggling, all of them looking in her direction as she walked by. Didn't these folks have anything better to do with their day?

Apparently not.

When she walked by the mercantile, Addie, the recently married storekeeper, came running out to greet her. Addie was never one to beat around the bush.

"You and that Aaron boy courting?" she asked point blank.

Susannah shook her head with exasperation as she stared at the wiry little lady. "Miss Addie, not you, too! I was just talking to the man, now everyone has me practically married off!"

Addie pulled out the pencil that was stuck in her gray hair and tapped it against her cheek. "Oh, but you couldn't do better than Bobby Joe! He'd make you a fine husband!"

"But I'm not interested in—"

"Who's getting married?" Harold Ray, Addie's new husband, asked as he walked over to the women.

"No one's getting married!" she said defensively, but they were looking at her as though they didn't believe her. "Oh, never mind!" she huffed and started walking off.

"Be sure and send us an invitation, ya hear?" Harold Ray called after her, causing Susannah to groan and walk faster.

After the fiasco in town, Susannah wasn't surprised to find both Patience and Rachel Stone knocking on her front door just minutes after she returned home. The three of them had become good friends in the past few months, and Susannah cherished their friendship. At the moment, she could really use their advice!

"Okay," Patience began without preamble as soon as she walked in the door. "We want to know what's going on!"

Rachel planted her hands on her hips and shook her head. "I was under the impression that you and Bobby Joe weren't getting along!"

Susannah bit back a smile and drawled, "Well, I do declare! It's certainly good to see y'all, too. And I'm doing just fine by the way. I know you would have asked me if you'd thought about it!"

Patience rolled her eyes and took Susannah's hand, while Rachel took the other one. As they pulled her to the sofa,

Patience told her, "That Southern belle act isn't going to work, Suz. We want the facts!"

Susannah laughed as they playfully shoved her down on the sofa and pulled two chairs close so that they could sit directly in front of her.

"Y'all are making the silliest fuss for nothing! There's nothing going on between Bobby and me!"

Rachel looked at Patience. "She's calling him Bobby," she observed, as if this were a major clue.

Susannah sighed. "All right, let me tell you what happened. But you've got to promise that this information will not leave the room."

Both ladies readily agreed, and Susannah told them the whole story.

After Susannah was finished, Rachel had tears in her eyes. "Oh, Susannah! What your poor sister must have been going through."

Patience, who was dabbing her own eyes with a lace hankie, asked, "How did Bobby Joe take it when you told him?"

"At first he didn't believe me. He's been carrying around bitterness for both my family and Leanna for so many years that he couldn't believe circumstances might not be what they seemed. But when we met today, he seemed more at peace, and he even apologized for ignoring me all these months."

Patience reached over and gripped her hand. "That's wonderful, Susannah. I know how you've been hurt by his actions."

Susannah shook her head. "He thought I'd talked his wife into leaving him. It wasn't his fault."

Rachel looked at her friend with keen eyes. Because of the hardships that she'd endured in her young life, she was more attuned to the feelings of others. "Susannah. . . ," she began, then she took a breath and continued. "Do you have feelings for Bobby Joe other than friendship?"

Susannah blushed and smoothed an imaginary strand of hair behind her ear. "Well. . .I. . . ," she stammered helplessly. She looked up at both of them and confessed, "Yes, I guess I do. I've tried not to, but I just can't seem to help myself. And I know he hasn't been a church-going man, but this may change things for him. He doesn't seem to blame God anymore. . .or me for that matter."

Rachel continued to look worried. "I hope that's true, Susannah, but you may need to give him more time."

Susannah forced a laugh. "You all are assuming that Bobby Joe would *want* to court me, which he doesn't! The man couldn't stand to look at me until yesterday!"

Patience made a tsk-tsk sound. "Now, I don't want to hear that! You are the prettiest girl in town! Who wouldn't want to court you?"

Susannah smiled at Patience gratefully. "Thank you, Patience." A thought suddenly crossed her mind and she frowned. "I may have another problem, though."

Rachel patted her on the knee. "You know what my husband always says! You can do all things through Christ!"

Susannah swallowed hard. "Well, I'm surely going to need His help, then, because I'm afraid I have another secret under my bonnet. This one Bobby Joe might not so readily forgive."

Patience waved away her concern. "Awww, it can't be that bad."

"You haven't heard it yet," Susannah answered faintly. "You see, I didn't come to Springton because of the teaching job. I came because my father sent me here to find a way to take Beth away from Bobby."

Both women gasped. Rachel spoke first. "Oh, that can't be true!"

"You're not really going to—" Patience blurted out.

"No!" Susannah quickly interjected. "You know I couldn't do a thing like that! I just went along with it because my father will not take no for an answer. And when he told me that I'd be teaching, I knew I had to come. Teaching has been my lifelong dream."

Patience frowned. "How much time did he give you to do this?"

"A year. I've already been here ten months."

"Oh dear," Rachel cried softly. "You've only got two months left! What will he do then?"

Susannah buried her face in her hands. "I don't know. I've ignored all his telegrams and letters, and I'm afraid he'll try to come here."

Rachel sat back in her chair and folded her arms. "Well, I don't think that will matter. You simply tell Bobby Joe the truth, and when your father arrives, let Bobby Joe deal with him. There's no way that he can take Beth anyway."

Susannah dropped her hands. "I'm afraid you don't know my father, Rachel. He can be ruthless when he wants something. Believe me, he'll find a way."

All her life Susannah had been in awe of, and a little bit afraid of, her father. And for the first time in her life she felt free. Free of his dictates and free of having to live up to his impossible standards. She tried not to think about being reunited with him; she could only pray that God would work it out.

Rachel seemed to read her thoughts, because she reached out her hands to both girls. "Why don't we say a prayer? I know God can give you the answers you need."

So together the girls bowed their heads, linked hands, and prayed. When they were finished, Rachel repeated her earlier advice, "Please let Bobby Joe know about your secret, Susannah. He'll take it better if it comes directly from you."

Susannah had her doubts about whether he'd take it well under any circumstances, but she nodded. "I'll just have to find the right time to do it, I guess."

"You'll do just fine, Suz," Patience comforted.

The three of them spent another half-hour together as Susannah served them coffee and cookies that she'd baked earlier. But when a knock sounded at her door, their conversation skidded to a halt.

"Well, for goodness sakes! Who can that be?" Susannah thought aloud.

"Oh, it's probably one of my children!" Rachel told them, getting up from her chair. "Just stay where you are and I'll go and check."

Patience and Susannah smiled at one another as Rachel raced to the front door. She and the reverend helped run an orphanage, and when Rachel referred to her "children," you never knew if she meant the orphans or her own three children.

They'd continued to chat, figuring Rachel would be away for a while, but were surprised to see her come back into the parlor.

"Uh. . .it wasn't my kids," she said with a secret smile playing about her mouth. "You have company, Susannah."

She stepped further into the room, and right behind her came Bobby Joe with his daughter, Beth.

"Beth! It's so good to see you!" Susannah exclaimed, jumping up from her chair and giving her niece a quick hug.

"Hi, Aunt Susannah. I couldn't believe it when Daddy told me we were coming to visit you, but I wasn't about to argue!

I sure didn't want him to change his mind," Beth said with her usual candor.

Susannah looked up at Bobby Joe and saw him wince. He had exchanged his dark suit for a neatly pressed white shirt and jeans. His hair was slightly jostled from the ride into town. To Susannah, he looked more handsome than she'd ever seen him. Maybe it was because he was standing in her house and smiling down at her.

"Hi, Bobby," she said, finding herself, for once in her life, at a loss for words. She felt like her tongue was tied in knots.

"Hello. I hope you don't mind us dropping by. I didn't know you'd be entertaining," he said hesitantly, looking at the other two women.

"Oh, don't worry about us!" Patience told him brightly as she scooped up her bag from the chair. "I was just on my way out, and Rachel was coming with me!"

"Oh! Yes! That's right. Patience and I were just leaving," Rachel added, suddenly understanding what her friend was up to.

"But. . .but I thought. . . ," Susannah sputtered as she followed them, suddenly nervous about being left alone with Bobby and his daughter.

The two women were already opening the front door. "We'll see y'all tomorrow!" Rachel told her as the door shut firmly behind them.

Quiet descended over her little house, and Susannah took a deep, fortifying breath. Gathering all her courage, she turned around with what she hoped was a believable smile and walked back into the parlor.

four

The moment Bobby Joe walked into Susannah's house, he'd begun having doubts about what he was planning to do. It wasn't that he hadn't been thinking of marrying again—he had. He'd even considered Patience Primrose Cutler a possible candidate, before she'd gotten engaged to the sheriff. She was nice and got along with Beth and his brothers, and that was basically all he required.

One thing he would never do was fall in love again. He didn't want to marry a woman because he loved her. He'd loved Leanna with everything in him, and it had hurt so bad when she'd left. He hadn't wanted to go on living.

The only thing that kept him going was the knowledge that Beth needed him. He never wanted to feel that way again.

Beth also needed a mother, and although his housekeeper did a great job of keeping the house running smoothly, it still needed a mistress. His brothers were all of marrying age, but none of them showed any inclination in that direction. So it was up to him.

But no matter how many reasons he came up with for carrying out his plan, he still felt guilty. Maybe it was because he felt so bad about having ignored Susannah all this time. Now here he was, about to ask her to make a life-changing decision.

As that thought hit him, he realized that it would make him seem selfish to come right out and tell her of his intentions today. Maybe he needed to spend time with her first, get to know her better. Then, when the time was right, he would ask her to marry him.

Having thought it all out, he was pleased with his decision to wait. As Susannah poured him a cup of coffee and brought Beth a cool glass of milk, he watched her easy and efficient movements. She certainly knew how to be a good hostess. Billy Ray had eaten at her house a few times and had mentioned that.

And another thing. With Susannah, a man certainly would never lack for conversation! This woman talked more than anybody he'd ever come across. That was good. She could talk for both of them, since conversation was never one of his strong points.

Yes, she would make the perfect wife. And a pretty one at that. Sure, he'd noticed how breathtakingly beautiful she was the first time he laid eyes on her. That had irritated him when they'd been at odds with one another; now he thought it an asset.

Yes, sir. Being married to this lovely woman would definitely fit nicely into his life. A marriage without all the emotional clutter. A marriage of convenience.

"So what brings you by?" Susannah asked, disturbing his thoughts. He looked into her light green eyes and felt an odd flutter in his chest. He convinced himself that he must be getting some sort of chest cold.

"I thought it would be nice to bring Beth over to see you. I explained to her that we had had a misunderstanding, and that was the reason she wasn't allowed to come and visit you before this," he said, sending a meaningful look. He didn't go into any details with Beth, since she hadn't known about her mother leaving in the first place. He'd always tried to speak only good things about Leanna to Beth, and since learning the truth, he was glad that he'd done so.

A look of understanding crossed her features as she smiled at Beth. "Ah. . .yes. We got everything settled between us."

Beth smiled radiantly. "I am so glad. I've so wanted to talk to you, especially about Mama. I've always wanted to know what she was like as a young girl."

"Well, don't you worry about that, sugar. I'll fill your head so full of stories, you won't be able to remember them all! Your mama and I had quite a few escapades in our younger days!"

Beth clapped her hands. "Oh, please tell me!"

Bobby Joe was pleased with how well they got along. "Now, Beth, we'll have plenty of time for that. Why don't you tell Aunt Susannah your good news."

"I'm going to be coming to your school soon! Daddy had to fire Mr. Copeland because he got dr—"

"Uh, Mr. Copeland was ill, so he had to leave," Bobby Joe amended quickly. He didn't want her to think he had shown poor judgment by hiring a drunk to tutor his seven-year-old daughter!

"Well, that's wonderful! There's not much left of the school year, but what there is, I'm sure you will enjoy!" Susannah gushed.

They chatted for another fifteen minutes or so, and then Bobby Joe saw that it was getting late. "We'd better be going so we won't be traveling back in the dark," he told Susannah as he stood up.

"Well, all right," Susannah replied with what sounded like a wistful sigh. "Thank you so much, Bobby, for bringing Beth by. You don't realize what this means to me." At that she reached out and took his hands in her own. "I'm so glad we're not enemies anymore."

That funny feeling in his chest was back, only this time it

was worse. He tried to clear his throat, but that didn't seem to help. He looked down at their hands and felt the softness of her skin against his rough palms, then looked back up at her mesmerizing green eyes.

Maybe he needed to see the doctor.

When he withdrew his hands, his chest felt a little better, and when he tore his eyes off of her and looked at his daughter, he felt *much* better. Just a coincidence, of course.

"Don't forget to ask her, Daddy!" his daughter prompted as she tugged on his shirtsleeve.

He looked at her in confusion for a moment, then remembered the plan that they'd come up with earlier.

"Oh, yeah!" He looked back at Susannah. "We wanted to know if you'd join us for dinner tomorrow night."

A happy glow seemed to emanate from Susannah's pretty face as she nodded quickly. "I'd love to. Thank you!"

He stared at her for a moment, admiring the way her eyes flashed with excitement. When he realized that she was looking at him expectantly, he knew he'd stared too long. "Oh. . . uh. . .that's great. I'll come around and pick you up about six, then."

She nodded and he quickly ushered his daughter out of the house to his waiting buggy.

It wasn't until he was a half-mile down the road that he began to relax. Shaking his head, he put a hand over his chest and coughed. *Yep*, he thought. *Must be getting a cold!*

❧

After three weeks of being around Bobby Joe, Susannah knew that she was irrevocably in love with the eldest of the Aaron brothers. Never would she have believed that being with him and getting to know him would be so wonderful. While it was true that Bobby usually didn't talk a lot, he always managed to find time to talk to her. He even opened up some about his life with her sister.

Susannah enjoyed hearing of their life together. She had loved her sister deeply and was glad that she had had this man to make her happy in the last years of her young life.

She was pleasantly surprised when Bobby Joe had continued to seek her company, whether it was to stroll about town or to have her over to his home for frequent dinners. Every Sunday they attended church together, and she could tell that, with the pastor's help, he was beginning to heal from all the bitterness that had gripped his life for so long. He always was attentive and kind—the perfect gentleman. The perfect beau.

Yet. . .he seemed to be holding something back from her. She knew he was fond of her, probably even liked her, but he never so much as hinted that he might love her. He didn't ever try to hold her hand, and never did she feel as though he wanted to kiss her. It was almost as if he just needed her friendship and nothing more.

But, every once in a while, she would catch him looking at her when he thought she wouldn't notice. It was a look of longing, almost as if he was looking at something he could never have.

That didn't make sense. He had to know she was in love with him; she'd never said the words, but her love showed through in every action and look that she gave him. It was something she was powerless to hide.

Perhaps after tonight there would be no need to hide anything. He told her he had something to talk to her about. . . something that could be important to both of them.

And she knew.

Bobby Joe Aaron was going to propose tonight! Would he tell her that he loved her, too? She didn't know. But she prayed it would be so.

When she heard the rattle of his wagon as he arrived, her excitement increased. After one last look in the mirror, she opened the door and ran out to meet him.

Tonight they dined alone, at a beautifully set table for two, on the porch just beyond the formal dining room. Azaleas in large pots produced a rainbow of colors all around them. White linen was spread over the round oak table, and two candles flickered romantically in crystal holders. The dishes were white china, and the food served upon them looked delicious.

But unfortunately, Susannah was too nervous to taste it. And when she became nervous, she talked. More than usual.

". . .and I can't even imagine how much work it is to grow such a beautiful garden. I mean, how many gardeners do you employ? I think the azaleas are so pretty this time of year, and it's a shame that they only bloom for a month or so, and the rest of the summer all you see is plain ol' green leaves. Don't you think—"

"Susannah," he called out softly, interrupting her nervous chatter.

Abruptly she stopped and stared at him. She wondered if he could actually hear her heart beating.

"I don't want to talk about the garden."

She swallowed. "Oh. What. . .what *did* you want to. . .to talk about?"

He smiled and leaned forward, resting his elbows on the table. "I want to ask you something, and you don't have to answer right away. If you need to think about it, I'll understand."

"My!" she said with a nervous smile. "This sounds serious."

"It is." He looked at her for a moment, then continued, "I wondered if you'd like to get married."

Susannah froze for a second. Something about how he'd asked didn't sound right. It sounded so. . .impersonal. "You. . .you want to get married?" she asked carefully.

He nodded seriously. So far, he had made no move to pull out an engagement ring or even to take her hand. Something definitely was not right.

"I think it would be a good arrangement for both of us. Beth needs a mother, and I know you love her like a daughter. . . . Am I right?"

Tears were beginning to clog her throat and her mind kept repeating the word "arrangement" over and over as if she couldn't make sense of it. "Yes," she whispered hoarsely.

He apparently did not notice her shock. "Now, I don't want you to worry about anything. This will strictly be a marriage of convenience."

"Convenience," she repeated dully.

"You could continue to teach or you can quit, it's up to you. But you've told me how much you enjoy it."

"Yes, that's true."

"My brothers love you, and so does my daughter."

Everyone but you, she thought. "I love them, too," she said out loud.

"If you decide this is what you want to do, then we can see Reverend Stone right away and have a quiet private ceremony."

After all, it's not real, right? "Okay."

For a moment he was silent, and she knew he was looking at her expectantly. But she couldn't look at him. Not yet. Not while the tears were fighting to fall from her eyes. Not while her heart was breaking in two.

"Uh. . .I think I have something in my eye. I'll be right back." With that, she stood up and walked quickly into the house.

After checking to see that he hadn't followed her, she wiped her eyes and leaned against the dining room wall. How did she not guess this was coming? How could she think he would want her as a real wife. . .in a real marriage?

She knew she was nothing like her sister. Perhaps he would never get over her death. Maybe a marriage of convenience was all he would ever be able to offer her.

Why did she have to love him so much? Why hadn't she just said no to her father when he wanted to send her here in the first place?

But crying over the past wouldn't help. She was in love with him, and she did want to marry him, even if it was in name only.

And she thought of something else. If she were married, her father couldn't force her to leave Springton. He would probably disinherit her like he'd done Leanna when *she'd* married Bobby. He would get mad and she'd probably never hear from him again.

Maybe she'd never have to tell Bobby her secret after all.

It was a selfish and self-serving thought, but there it was. In time, if she tried hard enough, maybe Bobby would come to love her.

Taking a fortifying breath, she picked up the skirts of her yellow satin dress and walked back outside. Bobby turned and gave her a searching look as she sat down.

"Did you get it out?"

At first she didn't know what he was talking about. "Uh. . . oh! Yes, my eye. It's better."

He nodded, although he looked skeptical. "Well, are you ready for me to take you home?" he asked while tossing his linen napkin on the table.

She reached out to put a hand on his arm when he made a

move to rise from the table. "I've made my decision."

He stopped and looked deeply into her eyes. "You don't have to. . ."

"I know, but I already know what I want." She smiled at him, even as she wondered if she was making the biggest mistake of her life. "The answer is yes. I think marriage is a good idea. For both of us."

Something flickered behind Bobby's eyes, but then it disappeared. He smiled and patted the hand that was on his arm. "I think we'll get along fine."

Relishing the feel of his hand on hers, she boldly turned her hand so that their palms were touching. "I do, too," she told him.

Please, God, she prayed silently as her future husband gallantly helped her up from her seat. *Please let this work out. Please let my love be enough for the both of us. . . .*

five

"I don't think you've thought this thing through!"

Susannah ignored the pang that shot through her heart at those words. Hadn't she been wondering the very same thing all week? Putting a smile on her face, she turned to Rachel. "Of course I've thought this through, Rachel. Believe me."

She saw Rachel and Patience, who were standing with her in one of Bobby Joe's guest bedrooms, give each other a worried look. "Susannah. . .are you in love with him?" Patience asked hesitantly. "I was hoping you two would start courting, but I had no idea you would want to get married so soon!"

Susannah turned back toward the full-length mirror and adjusted the long lace veil that fell across her face. It still stunned her to see herself in a wedding gown. Because they had decided to get married within the week, she hadn't had time to make a wedding dress of her own, so she was borrowing Rachel's. It was a lovely creation in satin and lace, and, after Rachel adjusted the seams a bit, it fit her perfectly.

But something was wrong, and she knew that Rachel and Patience could sense it. She wanted to open up to them and tell them that Bobby Joe didn't think of her as a real wife. She wanted to cry on their shoulders and tell them how she prayed that Bobby would come to love her as much as she loved him. But she just couldn't bring herself to do that. Too much Butler pride, she supposed.

So instead, she told them only half of the truth. "Of course I love him. I'm afraid I still haven't told Bobby about that teensy-weensy little secret yet, though."

"You haven't told him?"

"Oh, Susannah! That's not good!"

Both of the girls were talking at once, voicing their dismay. Susannah was glad, at least, that it had gotten them off the subject of the wedding.

"I just couldn't tell him," she confessed. "I mean, it may not even matter, you know. My father hasn't written me in weeks, and if he does, I'm just going to tell him that I'm not going to do it!"

Patience eyed her doubtfully. "I thought you said your father would stop at nothing to get his way. What if he shows up here?"

Susannah shrugged, keeping her horror of that thought well hidden. "I'll try to convince him not to."

Rachel walked up to her and took hold of both her hands. "Susannah, you can't start your marriage off with a secret standing between you. Bobby Joe loves you. He will understand."

Except Bobby *didn't* love her, and she had a feeling that he would never understand. She was barely a friend. In fact, she'd been his enemy longer than she had been in his good graces. No, he wouldn't understand. And when her father found out that she'd married Bobby, perhaps she would never have to tell him.

At that moment, the Aaron housekeeper stuck her head into the room and told them everyone was ready to start. Beth bounced in right after her, attired in a frilly blue dress, her dark brown hair in curls.

"Hi, Aunt Susannah! Are you ready to marry us?" she asked cheerfully.

Susannah gave her a genuine smile and reminded herself

that being a mother to Beth was definitely making this arrangement easier to go along with. "I sure am! I see you've picked some beautiful flowers. Did you get those from your garden?"

She held up the little basket she'd been holding. "Well, I picked one from our garden, and. . ." She looked a little sheepish as she confessed, "I also picked a couple from the rosebush in front of the school."

Susannah looked at her with mock sternness. "I usually make my students stand in a corner for picking my roses."

To her surprise, Beth jumped up and down gleefully. "Will I get to stand in the corner? I've always wondered what that would be like!"

Susannah's heart went out to the little girl. Since she had never attended school, she was still curious about it. But standing in a corner? Susannah had to laugh.

"Beth, standing in a corner is not a reward. It's a punishment."

Beth just shrugged. "How about cleaning the erasers?"

"That you can do! I never have very many volunteers for that."

"Can I also call you 'Mama'?"

Susannah drew in a quick breath. She didn't know how to handle that question. In her heart she would love to have Beth think of her as her mother. She knew Leanna would have approved. But Bobby was a different matter all together.

She sat down in a chair and pulled Beth near her. "Beth, we might need to talk to your daddy about that, okay?"

Beth sighed. "Well. . .okay. But no matter what he says about it, I'm still going to think of you as my mother."

Susannah hugged her close and blinked away the tears that were forming in her eyes. "And in my heart, you'll be my daughter," she whispered.

Patience patted her on the back, reminding her that everyone was waiting for her in the Aaron parlor. The ceremony would take place there, with only a few of their friends in attendance.

She hurriedly got up and gave her friends a quick hug. Then taking Beth by the hand, she walked out of the room.

She didn't know that he'd be waiting for her at the foot of the stairs. She was on the fourth step when she noticed him. He was wearing his beautiful black tuxedo, his hair slicked back smartly. She couldn't imagine there being a more handsome man anywhere. But it was his eyes that took her breath away. He was looking at her as if she were the most beautiful woman he'd ever seen. If she didn't know better, she would swear that there was. . .love in his eyes.

She knew that she would never make it through the wedding without crying.

&

For a moment Bobby's heart caught in his throat and he felt as though he couldn't breathe. She was so beautiful in satin and lace. It made him wonder if he was doing the right thing. What had he been thinking when he made this "arrangement" with her? Maybe he should have waited until love had grown between them and then had a real marriage.

Maybe. . . No! That was what he had been trying to avoid. He didn't want to love her. He didn't feel he could.

He held his hand out to her and watched as she shyly reached to take it. He looked at her once more, and this time he noticed the emotion on her face. She was looking at him the same way Leanna had gazed at him on their wedding day. It was as though Susannah. . .loved him.

He swallowed hard as he felt the warm, soft skin of her small hand. *Was* Susannah falling in love with him? He hadn't stopped to think about that happening. He had just assumed she would think of this marriage in the practical way he had. A marriage of convenience. They were friends—that was all.

But maybe she had her own reasons for marrying him.

Some inner bell was sounding in his head. The rational side of him was telling him to call this whole thing off. It wouldn't work. He hadn't really thought it through. He hadn't stopped to think about her feelings, about how Susannah would be affected by all this.

Every woman deserved romance and love. Every woman deserved a husband who loved her.

But he couldn't bring himself to stop this from happening. With her hand firmly tucked in his, he led her into the parlor, where the pastor and a small group of Bobby Joe's family members and their friends were gathered.

So much had happened in recent days. He'd finally managed to resolve his feelings about his wife leaving, becoming free of the bitterness that had gripped him for so many years.

He'd made his peace with God.

Maybe that was why he was willing to go through with the marriage. Marrying Susannah felt. . .*right*. . .in his heart.

But of course it wasn't because he loved her. He couldn't love her.

As he made the vow to love, honor, and cherish his bride, he wondered why the words seemed to ring true. And when Brother Caleb told him to kiss his bride, he held her sweet face between his palms, brushing her lips softly with his own. He tried to ignore the strange pull at his heart. He tried to shake off the feeling of happiness that swept through his soul. He tried to resist leaning down and giving her another kiss. He really tried, but he found himself kissing her again, this time lingering a little longer.

But it didn't mean anything. It couldn't.

❧

After the wedding, everyone was invited to the large dining room for finger foods and desserts. Susannah's head seemed to be swirling from the range of emotions that she'd experienced during the ceremony.

She was more confused than ever about the man who was her new husband. It was the way he had looked at her and then the way he had kissed her—not once, but twice! What did it mean? Was he beginning to have feelings for her?

She wanted so badly to hope that was true. But it was how he was acting now that made her doubt.

Gone was the smiling, gentle man who had held her hand and recited his vows as though he meant them. Gone was the man she'd felt so close to when they kissed.

In his place was the Bobby Joe Aaron she'd known since her arrival in Springton. He wouldn't even look at her as they stood together receiving congratulations from the few friends who were in attendance. He had become remote. Cold.

Was this behavior what she should expect from now on? Could they ever be friends?

As the evening wore on, Susannah became determined to speak to Bobby about it. She may have let her father control most of her life, but she never did it quietly. She always told him exactly how she felt about things. The only reason she gave into him was that he'd made her feel guilty. That was why she never left home to begin her career as a teacher, before coming to Springton. He'd made her feel so guilty about leaving him alone that she'd stayed.

It amazed her to realize that her father seemed to be doing just fine without her—as long as he thought she was collaborating in his kidnapping scheme.

No. She might be a pushover, but she didn't go down easily. Tonight she would have a heart-to-heart talk with Bobby and let him know that if they were going to be married, they would at least have to make an effort to be civil to one another. She didn't want to live the rest of her life having to tiptoe around this man and have to wonder every time he frowned at her.

If she couldn't have his love, she needed his friendship.

Rachel, Patience, and their husbands were the last to leave. Susannah hugged each of them and even had to assure Patience that she was all right.

Then it was just the two of them, standing in the large foyer. Susannah, still wearing her borrowed wedding dress, looked over at her new husband. She was surprised to find him staring at her, too, but then he dropped his eyes and stuck his hands in his pockets.

It's now or never! Susannah thought. "Could we talk, Bobby?" she asked hesitantly.

His eyes met hers again, and he didn't answer for a moment. But then he nodded his head. "Why don't we go into the library?"

She followed him into the large room and sat in the chair he offered; he took a seat in the chair opposite her.

Susannah took a deep breath. "I thought we could get a few things straight, Bobby," she stated calmly.

Bobby's placid expression turned into a scowl. "What things?"

"Don't you growl at me, Bobby Joe Aaron. That's the very thing I want to talk about! I thought we were friends. If I'm going to live under your roof, I expect you to treat me with kindness and respect. I don't want to wonder what's wrong with you every time you ignore me."

Bobby's eyebrow rose. "I wasn't ignoring you."

Susannah's eyes rolled incredulously. "I'll eat my fan if you weren't," she charged, sitting forward in her seat. "You've been treating me just like you used to, when you thought you hated me!"

Bobby's face became grim as he got out of his chair and stalked over to the large window. "I never hated you."

Susannah had to laugh at that statement. "You certainly didn't like me!"

"Susannah." He turned to look back at her. "Why are we discussing this? Isn't this just water under the bridge?"

Susannah stood and walked over to him. She wished that she knew what he was thinking. He seemed so remote, untouchable.

What in the world was wrong with the grumpy man?

When she reached him, she took his hand in her own and watched as he looked first at their hands and then at her. Then she spoke. "There're just two things we need to get straight here. Number one, if we are not going to tell people the truth about our little agreement, then we have to act like this is a normal marriage. You weren't acting like a happy bridegroom, by the way, at our reception.

"Number two, I agreed to this arrangement because I genuinely like you. But that's going to be short lived if you have that frown on your face every time you're in my presence!"

"What will you do? Send me to the corner?"

She threw down his hands in disgust. "I think my friends were right. I surely didn't take enough time to think this through. I must have been out of my little Southern mind to think we could get along together!"

He caught her arm as she tried to whirl away from him. "I was only kidding, Red," he teased, referring to her bright hair. "Did anyone ever tell you that you talk a lot?"

She jerked her arm from his grasp. "My name is not Red, it's Susannah; and yes, a few men who were lacking in gentlemanly manners may have mentioned the fact that I like to talk."

She was gearing up, ready for his next sarcastic comment, when he managed to take the wind right out of her sails.

"I'm sorry, Susannah. I didn't mean to be distant tonight."

She blinked and her mouth opened in surprise. "I surely don't understand you, Bobby. Sometimes I think there are two people living inside you."

He looked thoughtful for a minute, as if he were looking deep inside himself. "I guess I've lived with my pain and bitterness too long. It's hard not to fall back into that familiar attitude."

Susannah looked at his troubled expression and knew that he was trying to be open with her, trying to make things right. "Only God can totally remove the turmoil that you've been living with for so long, Bobby. And He's provided you with friends and family to help with the process. You just need to be surrounded by people who love and care for you."

An enigmatic look crossed his handsome features as he stared down at her. "What about you, Susannah? Are you going to love and care for me?"

She caught her breath for just a second as she tried to understand what he was asking. Did he really want to know how she felt, or was he testing her? With all her heart she wanted to tell him how much she was coming to love him, how much she wanted the marriage to be real.

But something made her hold back. To pour out her feelings and not have them returned would be devastating.

So instead, she gave him a bright smile and nodded her

head. "I love everyone, Bobby. Doesn't the Bible urge us to do so?" She innocently batted her eyes at him, causing him to laugh.

"Well put, Red. Friends?" he asked, holding out his hand.

She ignored his hand and reached up to hug him. "Of course we're friends. You can always be sure of that."

After a brief hesitation, she felt his arms come around her and hug her close.

Maybe they did have a chance after all, she thought. With God, all things are possible to those who believe. She prayed for the faith and patience to see it through.

six

Beth rose early and had dressed herself before Susannah was even up and about. Today was to be her first day of school, and Beth was bursting with excitement.

Bobby had offered to drive them, but Susannah knew he had much to do. So instead, he hitched up his buggy for them, then waved as Susannah and Beth left for town.

It was a new day, and Susannah had a fresh new outlook about everything. She still couldn't believe that she was a married woman. Already Mrs. Martin, their housekeeper, was coming to her and asking about how Susannah would like to run things, now that she was the mistress of the house.

Having run her father's house for so long, that part was easy. It was the interaction with Bobby that might get a little strange sometimes. He was her husband, yet he wasn't really. It was very confusing.

Susannah supposed that they would somehow get used to the idea. It certainly wasn't anything to worry about!

And after the school day was started, she didn't think about it at all. The children in her school ranged in age from five to sixteen, and except for a couple of rascals, most of them were well behaved and friendly. The first- and second-graders made Beth feel welcome and even invited her to sit and eat with them by the big oak tree in front of the school.

After school ended for the day, Susannah and Beth were sitting on the front steps of the school dusting the erasers—something Beth had been so excited to do—when the Aaron brothers rode up on their horses.

"Bobby Joe sent us to pick up Beth. He thought you might have some work to do," Daniel told her as all three of them jumped off their horses.

Beth responded before Susannah could. "I'm helping! I don't want to go home yet."

Billy Ray walked over and sat down beside her. "And a mighty fine job you're doing, too. I don't guess I've ever seen such clean erasers."

Beth glowed at his compliment. "Mama says I can clean the board next," she added.

All three brothers audibly sucked in their breaths. Beth didn't seem to notice, but Susannah did, and she was just as surprised as the brothers were at Beth calling her "Mama." She and Beth had never gotten around to asking Bobby about it, to see if it was all right.

"Uh. . .can you boys help me out with something inside? Beth, why don't you dust off the rest of those erasers?" Susannah got up from the steps and waited for the brothers to follow her.

Susannah began to try to explain as they walked into the large classroom. "I didn't ask Beth to call me Mama. I told her she needed to ask Bobby about it, but. . ." She trailed off with a helpless shrug of her shoulders. Frankly, she wasn't sure how the boys felt about her or how they would react. The only one she'd ever talked to was Billy Ray. Tommy and Daniel were something of a mystery to her.

Billy Ray was quick to assure her. "We don't care about that. If Beth feels so close to you, then I think it's for the best."

"Susannah, what we'd really like to know is what this whole 'marriage' thing is all about," Tommy said without mincing words. His voice was curious and a little confused.

"Yeah," Daniel chimed in. "We know that he stopped being mad at you and all, but the next thing we knew, y'all were married! He didn't even court ya!"

Billy glared at his brothers before he looked back at Susannah. "Susannah, we don't mean to pry, and if it's none of our business, well, just tell us so. We're all just a little confused by this sudden turnaround, is all. When we ask Bobby Joe about it, he just shrugs it off."

Susannah's mind whirled as she tried to come up with a reasonable explanation, but she couldn't. And to be honest, she was tired of keeping secrets. "Actually, I think it was something you all said to him."

"What?" they all exclaimed in unison.

Susannah nodded. "He told me that one of you had mentioned the fact that I was practically family and that it would seem all right if he were to court me. Well, he went a step further and decided that he needed a wife more than he needed a woman friend, because of Beth. He thought that I would be a good mother substitute for her."

A deafening quiet descended over them as they began to comprehend what Susannah was suggesting.

"He married you because Beth needed a mother?" Daniel asked, trying to sort the whole thing in his mind.

Susannah just nodded.

Tommy shook his head. "That's downright crazy, if you ask me!" He looked at Daniel. "Did Bobby Joe get hit on the head out at the sawmill recently?"

Daniel shrugged his shoulders. "I don't think so, but something must have addled his brain. Meaning no disrespect, Ma'am," he said to Susannah hurriedly, "but Bobby Joe never does anything on the spur of the moment. He does everything in a rational manner."

"Well, this ain't any kind of rational manner that *I've* ever seen!" Tommy offered.

Billy Ray, who had been watching Susannah while the other brothers were talking, spoke up at last. "What about you, Susannah? You told us why Bobby Joe married you, but you didn't say why you married him. Why would you marry someone who's been nothing but nasty to you this whole year?"

Susannah could feel a blush rise on her cheeks. She quickly looked down and smoothed her blue cotton skirt. "Well, I did it for Beth. I wanted nothing more than to be with her. And being her stepmother was like a dream come true for me." It was only half the truth, and the men seemed to sense it.

"That blush that matches your hair is telling another story, if you ask me!" Tommy observed bluntly.

"Tommy, don't you remember any of the good manners that our mother taught us?" Billy scolded.

"I don't know, Billy. I think Tommy's right. I saw how she looked at him at the wedding. It looked like true love to me," Daniel inserted.

"I was too busy looking at our eldest brother! Did you happen to catch his face? He had the look of a hound dog gazing at a rabbit darting across the meadow. Believe me, he looked besotted."

"Gentlemen, I do believe you are pulling *my* leg now!" Susannah charged in her best teacher's voice. She had her hands on her hips, her foot was tapping rapidly, and she had a no-nonsense look on her face.

Tommy held up his hand. "I promise you, I'm telling the truth as I saw it!"

"Well, that certainly isn't a promise that'll hold much

water," a deep voice drawled from the doorway.

Everyone turned in surprise to see Bobby Joe standing there staring at them.

Susannah's heart flew to her throat as she wondered just what he'd heard. But when Bobby asked what exactly it was that Tommy had promised, she relaxed.

"Oh, these guys were just kidding around with me. I tell you, Bobby, you have three charming brothers!" she said quickly.

Bobby Joe just grunted. "That's your opinion. I think they're just plain ornery!"

The brothers began to protest, but he held up his hand. "I sent ya'll here to pick up Beth, not to give my wife here a hard time!"

Susannah's eyes flew to Bobby's when she heard the word "wife" slide easily off his tongue. He met her gaze and gave her a playful wink that made her smile.

There he goes surprising me again, she thought, a little exasperated. Would she ever understand the man?

"Aw, we're just getting to know her a little, is all!" Tommy told him.

"Uh-huh. Well, now that you've had your little chat, could y'all do as I asked and take Beth home?"

Daniel scowled and thrust his hat back on his head. "How come you can't take her? We just might want to go over and see the new prisoner the sheriff has locked up in the jail. Billy Ray told us he stole a couple of Harold's horses down at the stables!"

"Go see the prisoner tomorrow. Today, I thought I'd take Susannah to her old house and finish packing up her things."

The brothers grumbled as they left the room. Beth ran in and handed Susannah the erasers. "Can I clean the boards tomorrow? My uncles told me I have to leave." She looked so concerned over neglecting her new duties, that Susannah had to bend down and give her a hug.

"Of course it's all right. The boards will be here tomorrow. They're not going anywhere."

She turned to her dad then and asked him the question that Susannah had been dreading. "Daddy, is it all right if I call Aunt Susannah 'Mama'? She told me I had to ask you, but I said you wouldn't mind."

Susannah held her breath as a look of pain crossed his features, and then it was quickly masked. He reached out and smoothed her shiny hair back with a gentle hand. "Of course I don't mind, sweetheart. I think every little girl needs someone to call Mama, and you couldn't ask for a better mama than your aunt Susannah."

"I think so, too! Thanks, Daddy." She hugged him quickly and waved to Susannah. "Bye, Mama!" And with that she ran out of the room, her step full of youthful enthusiasm and joy.

"Thank you, Bobby. When she asked me, I wasn't sure how you'd feel about it."

He waved off her concern. "I'm not totally unfeeling, Susannah. We're married now, so it's just natural that she'd want to call you Mama."

Susannah blew out an exasperated breath. "I know you're not an unfeeling man, Bobby. I think you have a whole lot of feelings just swirling around in you that you never let anyone see."

He seemed uncomfortable with this observation. "Aw, that's just women-talk. I'm just a regular guy, like anyone else."

Susannah shook her head. Men, she had always observed, never like to discuss their feelings. "Well, regular guy, are you ready to mosey on over to the house? I do have just a few more things to pack."

It only took about an hour to pack the rest of her belongings and load them on the wagon. And when she thought they were ready to go, he surprised her by pulling out a large basket from the front of the wagon. "Mrs. Lewis packed us a basket of sandwiches and dessert. Since the furnishings that go with the house are still here, we can just eat on the table."

Susannah took the basket from him and disagreed. "I'd rather put a blanket on the floor in the parlor! It will be like having a picnic!"

Bobby shook his head and muttered something under his breath that sounded like "Women!" and then walked back to the wagon to get a blanket.

Susannah helped him lay out the blanket, and soon they were sitting together, feasting on the delicious ham and cheese sandwiches that the housekeeper had made for them.

"See? Isn't this more fun?" Susannah enthused.

"Well, at least we don't have ants to contend with."

"Oh, phooey! Would it hurt to just admit that you like doing something a little silly occasionally?"

He smiled and looked at her curiously for a few moments. "You know, you're so different from the way your sister was."

Intrigued, she asked, "How so?"

He wiped his mouth as he shrugged. "Leanna was so practical about everything. A real no-nonsense lady. If we'd eaten on the floor like this, it would be because the table had broken in two. She was a lot like me, I guess."

Susannah's spirits sank at hearing that. She knew exactly how Leanna was, and it was because they were so different that they'd gotten along. Their differences kept them from being bored with each other.

"I guess you must think I'm the silliest woman around,

then. Not everybody would eat on a floor when there's a perfectly good table just sitting there."

"Actually, I like it that you're so different from me. You'll liven up our drab little household."

Relief bubbled up in her chest, and she couldn't help but smile. "Well, I'm glad I can be of some use!" she teased as she reached over to brush a piece of bread from the side of Bobby's mouth with her napkin.

He took her hand before she could pull away. "It's more than that, Susannah. I know I haven't done a good job of showing it, but I appreciate your taking a chance by marrying me. I know it wasn't fair to you, and I'm grateful."

As Susannah savored the feel of his strong hand as it held her own, she wished again that he would fall in love with her, just a little. Her sister must have realized just how blessed she was to be loved by such a man. *If only. . . ,* she thought. *If only. . .*

But her musings were stopped short as he continued speaking.

"I've wondered, too, how your father has reacted to your marrying me. I know he wasn't thrilled when Leanna and I eloped. He must have been furious."

At once, her eyes fell from his. She was never good at hiding her feelings, and he must have noticed. When she tried to pull her hand away, he held fast.

"You didn't tell him?" he asked incredulously. "I was under the impression that you and your father were close."

"We were. . .are! I just couldn't gather up the courage to wire him." She finally pulled her hand away. "But I'll get around to it, in my own timing."

Bobby just shook his head at her. "Why don't we go down to the telegraph office and wire him today?"

Susannah knew she would have to tell her father sooner or later. She just thought it would be later. She still had a few weeks to go before her year was up, and she had planned to tell him at the end of it.

Well, apparently today would be the day.

With a big sigh, Susannah nodded in agreement. She supposed it didn't matter. Her father would be so furious with her that he would probably disinherit her like he did Leanna. She would receive a note from his solicitor, then that would be that.

Or would it? No matter how much she tried to reassure herself, the doubts would not go away.

The fact of the matter was, her father did not want to be left without a legacy. She and Beth were all he had left. Susannah had a feeling that he would not give up so easily.

seven

Susannah and Bobby Joe settled into a comfortable routine. She went to her teaching job every day with Beth, then he usually had one of the brothers drop him off at the school to drive them home.

Slowly he was becoming more open and a lot more talkative, so much so that she could imagine he was becoming the charming man he once had been—the man her sister had fallen head-over-heels in love with.

She herself was more in love with him than ever. And although she didn't know how he felt about her, she imagined that he cared for her in some fashion. He showed it whether they were in public or in private. Always attentive, always courteous.

He attended church with her each Sunday, also. She'd been told by Patience and Rachel that everyone was remarking on what a perfect couple they were and how much in love they looked. She would glimpse the secret smiles of the older women and the envious ones of the younger women.

If they only knew. She would be pitied instead of envied.

Sometimes she pitied herself. At those times she would remind herself that she'd walked into the agreement with her eyes open. If she wasn't happy now, it was her own fault.

But tonight, she had reason to hope. Bobby had arranged for them to have a special dinner, apart from the rest of the family in the formal dining room.

He had seemed so mysterious about everything. He would

only say that he had something to discuss with her.

Susannah would not let herself hope. If she did, she would imagine him asking her to be his wife in truth, setting aside their "convenient" arrangement.

It probably had something to do with Beth. Of course, that's what it was.

"You look lovely, Red," Bobby said, his voice echoing softly in the large room. He used that nickname frequently now, and she'd given up trying to correct him. She'd even grown to like it.

Susannah turned away from the window, which was framed by a heavy red velvet curtain, and faced him as he sauntered into the room. They'd both dressed formally tonight—she in her best green satin dress and he in his dashing black suit.

"You look rather dapper yourself, Mr. Aaron," she answered lightly.

He walked over to her and took her hand, leading her over to the dining table that was beautifully set with fine china and silver. Two long, tapered candles had been set on one end of the table, casting the room in a soft glow.

Gallantly he held out her chair, then took the one at the head of the table, just catty-corner from her.

Mrs. Lewis entered the room carrying aromatic dishes. Susannah was just sorry she couldn't enjoy it. She ate as much as she could, but her stomach was in knots. The waiting and the wondering were killing her!

Silently she prayed that God would give her peace, that she could accept whatever he had to say. And she did feel better after that.

When the coffee was being served, Susannah could wait no longer. "Bobby, are you going to keep me in suspense all night? Shame on you for being so mysterious."

Bobby smiled at Susannah's exasperation. He knew the wait had been difficult for her, but he had to see how she responded to him, with the dinner and all, before he told her what was on his mind.

For three weeks they'd lived together as friends and companions. He found himself yearning to spend more and more time with her. Even when she was teaching school or visiting friends, he missed her. After the first week, he realized that she was on his mind most of the time, and his feelings were growing stronger.

He also knew he could no longer deny what he was feeling—nor could he blame it on a cold! He was head over heels in love with his wife.

And there stood his dilemma. He had entered into an agreement that no longer was satisfactory to him. He wanted them to have a real marriage, a loving relationship. He wanted this lovely woman with the pretty freckles across her nose to bear his children; he wanted the two of them to grow old together.

He thought she wanted the same thing, but he wasn't totally sure. Tonight, when he'd walked into the room and had seen the love shining in her eyes, he knew. He knew that she loved him.

"I have something important to ask you, Red," he answered her, finally.

"All right," she replied breathlessly.

He reached over to hold her hand. "I wanted to talk to you about ending our agreement."

Susannah gasped. "What? You want a divorce?"

He held fast to her hand as she tried to pull away. "No! I don't want a divorce! I want just the opposite," he was quick to assure her.

She seemed to relax, but she was still frowning at him. "But we're already married, Bobby."

Bobby gave a self-conscious laugh and shook his head. "I'm not doing this very well. What I'm trying to say is. . ."

A sharp rap at the dining-room door interrupted him. Before he could say "Enter," the door burst open. Mrs. Lewis ran into the room, looking harried.

"I'm sorry, Mr. Bobby, but there's a man who insists on seeing both you and Miss Susannah," she burst out, nearly in tears.

Alarmed, Bobby Joe and Susannah jumped up from their chairs. "It's all right, Mrs. Lewis. I'll see who it is," he said as he started toward the door.

He had almost reached it, when a richly dressed, gray-haired man walked into the room. His stance was haughty, his eyes narrowed.

Bobby Joe had to work to keep the distaste from showing on his face as he stared at Winston Butler, his two-time father-in-law.

"Daddy!" Susannah cried. But it was not a happy exclamation; it was filled with fear.

Bobby knew that Winston Butler was a hard man to get along with, but he didn't think he was one to be feared—and certainly not by his own daughter.

"I honestly thought that you'd tried to waggle out of our deal, girl! But when I received your telegram, I knew that you'd been a busy little bee." He laughed with glee. "I couldn't have come up with a better plan myself. My, if you aren't a chip off the old block!"

Bobby strained to understand the man's words as his wife went whizzing past him. She grabbed Winston by the arm and tried to pull him from the room.

"Daddy. . .you must be tired! Why don't you just get

yourself upstairs, and I'll find you a room!" she told him with a brightness that sounded false to Bobby's ear.

"Susannah, I want to know what he's talking about. What does he mean by your 'plan'?" Bobby Joe demanded. He had a very bad feeling about Winston Butler being here.

"Oh, Bobby, he's not making any sense right now. He'll sound better after he's rest—"

"I'm not going anywhere, Daughter! And quit pulling on my coat!" He jerked his arm from Susannah's grasp and marched over to where Bobby Joe stood. "Game's up anyway. Don't worry, Sugar, Daddy's taking over now." He smiled at Bobby with such a slick, triumphant smirk that it made Bobby Joe feel sick.

"Daddy, please. . . ," Susannah cried, to no avail.

"Why don't you start from the beginning, Butler. You're just bursting to tell me anyway."

"I've come for my daughter and my granddaughter."

Bobby Joe wasn't sure he'd heard the man right, and if he had, Susannah's father had to be out of his mind. "I beg your pardon?" His voice was low and dangerous.

Winston Butler paid him no heed. "I sent Susannah here to bring Beth back to Charleston."

Bobby Joe's heart was pumping fiercely as he struggled to comprehend just what was happening. He looked at his wife, the woman he'd grown to love. . .and trust.

"Susannah?" He begged her with his eyes to clear up this matter, to tell him what her father was saying was untrue.

But she was crying. . .and looking very, very guilty.

"Bobby, let me explain. It's not what—"

"Not what I think?" he practically yelled at her, his heart breaking into a million pieces. "What is it I am supposed to think, Susannah?"

She ran to him and tried to grab his arm, but he shook her loose. She stepped back and clasped her hands in a pleading gesture. "He did send me here, but I never planned to do what he says. I didn't marry you because of what he wanted me to do."

"That's right," he barked sarcastically. "You married me out of the goodness of your heart—because you loved my daughter. Isn't that what you told me?"

"I married you because I love you, Bobby," she whispered hoarsely, the tears falling in streams down her cheeks. It made his heart hurt to see her cry, yet he, too, felt like crying. How could he have been so blind?

"If you had loved me, you would have told me the truth," he stated, enunciating clearly.

"Susannah, what in the world is wrong with you? There isn't any need for all this sniveling. You have a legal right to his daughter now. Let's go and be done with it!" Butler broke in with a thread of impatience evident in his deep voice.

Susannah whirled and faced him. "I did not marry Bobby so that you could get your hands on Beth. I decided not to go along with your stupid plan right after I got here. Why did you think I never answered your letters? There's no way I'd ever want Beth to live in that big empty house with you and not with her father."

"I won't have you disobey me, Susannah. We had a deal, and I'm here to see that it's carried through."

"You'll get my daughter over my dead body, Butler. Now get out of my house and take your daughter with you!" He thrust an angry finger at the doorway as he glared at Winston Butler. He wouldn't look at his wife. He couldn't. He just wanted her gone.

"No! Bobby, please listen—"

Winston Butler interrupted her again. "You don't know who you're messing with, Aaron. I'll drag you through every court in the land, and believe me when I say that I'll come out the victor!"

"You won't without my help, Daddy," Susannah said, her words causing a stillness to settle in the room.

"Now, you hold on a minute. . ."

"No, you hold on! I'm not going with you and I'm not going to let you take Beth. This is our home. . .we're *both* staying." Susannah thrust her chin stubbornly into the air, and Bobby had to admire her for standing up to him. If that truly was what she was doing. It could be a trick.

"You stay here, and I'll write you out of my will!"

"Do it. I'm staying."

Butler's jaw worked furiously as he tried to reign in his temper. "Then I'll go. But you haven't heard the last of me, Aaron. I'll be back. And next time, be prepared to lose." With that, he turned and stalked to the door.

"I'll be waiting," Bobby called to his back. He was so angry. . .so hurt. And to think he had been about to tell her that he loved her. What a fool he'd been.

"Bobby, why don't we sit down and talk this out. Once you hear what I have to say, I think it'll help." She tried once more to take his arm, but again he backed away from her. A hurt expression crossed her face, and fresh tears filled her eyes.

"Nothing you can say will change anything. I was wrong to trust you. I won't make that mistake again." He moved away from the table and walked to window. He looked out as his hands gripped the window's frame. "Please pack your belongings and go. I'm sure that Patience or Rachel can take you in, or you can go back to your old house. I really don't care. Tomorrow you can buy a ticket back to Charleston."

"You have to listen to me, Bobby. Please. . .I love you. . . ."

"Stop saying that!" he growled as he closed his eyes tightly. "Don't make a scene, Susannah. Just leave."

After a moment of silence, she spoke, her voice thick with tears. "I'll leave your house, Bobby, but I won't leave Springton. I'm not going to give up on us, either."

She sniffed and he opened his eyes to see her reflection in the window pane. She was wiping her cheeks with her lace hankie. "I'm so sorry for not telling you why I came to Springton. My friends told me to, but I kept putting it off. After a while, it was too late. Too much time had passed. I didn't want to ruin our fragile rela—"

"Good-bye, Susannah," he broke in. He couldn't hear anymore. It hurt too much to listen.

He watched as she stood there a moment more, and then she straightened, squaring her shoulders. It was something he'd seen her do often, a show of determination.

"Good night, Bobby. I'll talk to you soon."

She walked out and closed the door behind her. The sound seemed to reverberate through his body, piercing his heart. It sounded so final.

But what worried him the most was his daughter.

What was he going to tell Beth?

eight

As soon as Patience opened her door, Susannah started to tearfully explain what she was doing there.

"Oh, Patience. . .I'm so sorry to bother you, but I didn't know what else to do. It's awful, just awful. I don't know why I didn't listen to you and Rachel! I tell you, I'm the silliest thing to ever walk on this earth! If I'd. . .if I'd just told him, then he might have forgiven me. But I didn't. And even if I had told him, he probably wouldn't have forgiven me anyway, so I guess all I did was delay the inevitable."

She dropped her face into her hands. "Ohh! What am I going to do? Where am I going to go? I'm just so. . ."

"Susannah! It's all right! Whatever it is, I'll help you—you know that," Patience soothed, putting her arms around her and patting her back in a motherly gesture. She had a sleep bonnet on her head and was covered from her neck to her toes in a white cotton nightgown.

"What's the matter with Susannah?" Lee asked, coming to the door. Yawning, he rubbed his eyes and fingered the buttons on his shirt. He was dressed in striped pajamas, and his hair was sticking up in all directions.

"I'm not sure, Lee. But I don't think it's good." She leaned away from Susannah and held her by the shoulders.

"Susannah, are you trying to tell me that Bobby Joe kicked you out of the house?"

Susannah managed a small nod before she burst into another torrent of tears.

"Oh, dear!" She looked at Lee helplessly, then took Susannah firmly by the arm. "Come on in. I'll fix you some hot tea. Then you can explain it all to us."

After she'd swallowed a couple of sips of the hot tea, she managed to stop crying. She felt so embarrassed to have imposed on her friend like this, but she had no one else to turn to. She supposed she could go back to the little house where she'd lived before; it had furniture, and no one was living in it.

But tonight she didn't want to be alone. She had to have someone to talk to. So she told Patience everything that had happened.

"Oh, Susannah! How could your father do such a thing?" Patience cried.

Susannah shook her head, feeling miserable. "He's capable of doing just about anything to get what he wants. I'd foolishly convinced myself that he would just give up and leave me alone. I should have known he'd never do that."

Patience patted her friend's hand. "Well, I don't think he's going to get anywhere where Bobby Joe's concerned. Bobby Joe would fight to the death to keep him from getting his daughter."

"I know that. He can't really do anything anyway, since I told him that I wouldn't help him. Can you believe that? He really thought that I married Bobby just so I could have some legal right to Beth!" Susannah shook her head in disgust. "But that's not the worst of it. . . ."

Patience eyed her warily, disbelief etched on her face. "It gets worse?"

"Bobby and I were having a special dinner when my father interrupted. He was about to tell me that he loved me. I know he was."

Stunned, Patience sat for a minute before she asked delicately, "Uh. . .Susannah? If Bobby has never told you he loved you, why did you marry him?"

Dramatically, Susannah buried her head in her hands again. "It was to be a marriage of convenience," she wailed, the words muffled and nearly unintelligible. Patience reached up and pulled her hands back so that she could understand.

"Did you say 'convenience'?"

"He thought that since I was already practically family, I'd make a good mother for Beth." But as she said the words, she realized just how sad that sounded. And from the pitying look on her friend's face, apparently she thought so, too.

"Why didn't you tell Rachel and me?"

"I was too ashamed that I was willing to marry him under those circumstances. But Patience, I was so much in love with him, I would have married him under *any* circumstances."

Patience propped her hand under her chin and sighed. "I know all about being in love with someone who doesn't love you in return. I thought that Lee would never see the light!" Then she looked pointedly at Susannah. "But he did. And I don't believe that God wouldn't want the same for both of you. Marriage is sacred. We just need to pray about it; God will help."

Susannah nodded. "I know. But Bobby turned away from God before because of his bitterness. I hope he doesn't do the same this time, too, because of my stupidity."

Patience held up her hand. "Let's not talk like that! We have to have faith." She rose from the table. "Now, let's get you to bed. Tomorrow, you'll be thinking more clearly and maybe will figure out a way to talk to Bobby."

Susannah got up from her seat. "You're right," she said with a teary smile. "Perhaps a little shut-eye would do me good."

All the sleep in the world couldn't have prepared Susannah for what she would have to face after a fitful night.

At a little past five in the morning, a frantic knock sounded on Lee and Patience's front door. Susannah, who'd been lying in bed staring at a dark ceiling after a restless night, jumped out of bed and listened at the door. She heard Patience open the door and speak to someone with a deep voice.

She was in the process of donning her robe when Bobby Joe burst through her bedroom door. He didn't look happy. His hair hadn't been combed, and his face was dusted with morning whiskers.

"Bobby! What—" she began.

"Where is she?" he demanded, grabbing her by the arm.

"I don't understand. . . ."

"Beth! What did you do with her?"

"Bobby, I don't know what you're talking about. Are you trying to tell me that Beth is missing?"

He gripped her arm tighter, but when he saw her wince, he let go. She saw that he was trying to calm himself, but he looked as if he were on the verge of falling apart. "I went in to check on her this morning, before I went to the sawmill. Her bed was empty. I need to know if you and your father have kidnapped her."

Susannah gasped. "If Beth is missing, Bobby, I had nothing to do with it. I haven't seen my father since he interrupted our dinner last night."

"Stop the lies, woman, and tell me where your father took her!"

Anxiously, Susannah tried to think of where her father might have taken Beth—it was almost inconceivable that he was capable of doing it at all. Regardless, she didn't know if her father had stayed in town or not. "I don't know," she told him. When he let out an impatient breath, she snapped, "Look, Bobby, I told you that I had no idea he was coming, all right? Are you sure that my father took her?"

He stared at her as if he were looking at a stranger. "You're unbelievable, you know that? Your little secret has been revealed, Susannah. You came to this town with the evil plan to take my daughter from me. No wonder you were so eager to tell me about Leanna. Or was any of that even true?"

It tore her heart in two to see him so bitterly against her. Before, it had made her sad that he didn't want to have anything to do with her. Now things were different. Now she loved him, and for a little while, she believed, he had loved her back.

"Of course it was true, Bobby. I told you that I had never planned to go along with my father. I had nothing to do with this; please believe me," she pleaded with everything that was in her.

But he ignored her plea.

"If he hurts her. . ." His voice cracked, and he turned away from her and raked a hand through his thick hair. "She better be all right," he spat out, then turned to leave the room.

"Wait, Bobby! I'll go with. . ."—she heard the front door slam shut—". . .you," she finished lamely.

She didn't waste any time. She quickly dressed and went to tell Patience what was happening. Lee set up her buggy for her, and Susannah headed out toward the Springton Inn. If her father was close enough to grab Beth, he probably was staying there.

Bobby had obviously had the same idea, because he was coming out as she was entering the inn. "We're too late. He's gone."

"Did they say where he'd gone?"

Bobby shook his head. "They said that he'd hired a private coach to take him to Charleston. All I know is that he's got an early start on us. Somewhere along the way, he'll probably catch a train."

"Why wouldn't he just take the train here in town?"

"Because he knew that I'd have the law stop him at one of the train stops. I talked to Sheriff Cutler before I left, and he's got men on the lookout, but we don't know what road he took or how much he'll go out of the way to elude us."

She looked at his weary face and hated the worry that she saw brimming in his blue-green eyes. "So what are you going to do?"

Suddenly his face grew hard and he glared at her. "What do you care, Susannah? Or perhaps you have more secrets to share. What do you want next, my business? My house?"

"I don't want anything but your forgiveness, Bobby. Please let me help find her. I love her, too," she pleaded, wishing she could make him believe her.

"Stay out of my business, Susannah. My family no longer concerns you," he told her harshly, as he brushed past her.

"No, I won't!" she screamed after him, causing the few people who were out and about to freeze and stare at both of them.

"Would you keep your voice down?" he hissed.

"I am still part of this family. I am your wife, and no matter how much you wish differently, that's the way it is." She marched up to him and poked him in the chest with her finger. "So let's get something straight. You're going to go after my father and I'm going with you, and that's that! He'll deal with me better than with you anyway."

Bobby just stood there staring at her, his hands on his hips.

It was a standoff—like two gunslingers waiting for each other to draw. Some of the anger began to drain from his eyes. "You'll just be in the way."

"I don't think so!" She, too, had her hands on her hips.

He stood for a moment more, his jaw clenched tightly. Then his shoulders slumped in defeat. "Come on," he growled. He turned and stalked to his buggy. "Anyway, when we find him, you can just stay with him. Then I won't ever have to see you again!" he yelled as he walked, throwing his arms up in the air.

Determined not to let his words get to her, she ran after him.

But when he started to climb up, he looked around with a scowl. Following his gaze, she noticed that more people had come out to watch their dispute. Most of the folks who knew Bobby Joe probably thought he had lost his mind. For a man who was gentle-spoken if he spoke at all, this shouting match was a big step out of character for him.

"Show's over," he barked to all who were listening. He then jammed his hat lower on his head and jumped into the wagon.

They rode out of town to the applause and whistles of the townspeople.

"See what your little display has caused?" Bobby Joe barked. "The whole town's going to be talking about it for days."

Susannah turned to him with an incredulous look. "And the fact that you threw me out of your house wouldn't have caused any talk? Did you think about the scandal that would bring about?"

"No, I didn't. I wasn't thinking about anything but that secret you've been keeping from me."

Susannah stared at his strong face and had to stop herself from reaching out to him. "I'm sorry, Bobby. I don't know what else to say."

"Well, that's a first."

Her face reddened at his barbed words. She knew she talked a lot. She just didn't know that it bothered him. "Better than not talking at all," she shot back childishly.

Apparently he thought her words weren't even worth commenting on. Bobby just shook his head and looked away.

They sat there in silence for a moment. But silence wasn't something that Susannah did well. If she were talking, she somehow thought she was making progress. "So! What's the plan?" she asked with an overly bright tone.

She saw his jaw working in frustration. Just as she loved to talk, Bobby would rather brood. "We're going to go get supplies and then catch the stage over in Shreveport. I thought we might have a chance of catching up with him if we stayed off the train. It's probably wishful thinking, but I have to try."

She nodded and looked toward the sawmill that was coming into sight. She felt she had to reassure him once more. "Bobby, he won't hurt her. He's overbearing, rude, and selfish, but he would never harm his own granddaughter. In his own strange way, he loves her. She's kin."

She saw him clench his eyes for a moment, then open them and stare straight ahead. "She's not with her family, Susannah. What if she thinks I let Butler take her? What if he tells her that?"

It was likely her father would do that, she knew.

Bobby was right The sooner they got Beth back, the better. "Let's just keep trusting in God. He'll take care of her."

"I pray that you're right because I'll never forgive you if something happens to her. Every bit of this is your fault. Every bit," he said savagely. His statement seemed to echo in the early dawn air.

His words pierced her heart like the point of an arrow. But

he had every right to feel this way. She wouldn't be able to forgive herself, either, if Beth were harmed in any way.

After all, what happened really *was* entirely her fault.

nine

It had been about ten in the morning when they reached Shreveport. Daniel had ridden along with them so he could take their wagon back after they'd departed on the stagecoach.

Bobby Joe had fallen into silence after they'd reached the house, and Susannah had been grateful to have Daniel to talk to on the way to Shreveport. But now, on the stage, it was just the two of them—except for one other passenger, an elderly man. Bobby had taken a little time to dress in a clean chambray shirt, a brown coat, and dark blue cotton pants. Susannah still wore the yellow calico dress that she'd thrown on at Patience's house, and she knew that her red hair must look a fright. She'd pulled it back in a ponytail, and a crooked one at that. It wasn't fair that Bobby looked sharp and neat, when she must look like a pauper.

She sighed, then pulled up the dusty shade to look out the window. This was not going to be a pleasant trip. If Bobby continued to ignore her, she would just go nuts! There had to be something she could say. . .something she could do.

Suddenly she realized what she'd forgotten to do—she hadn't prayed. She'd been trying to sort out the whole mess by herself and hadn't stopped to ask God for guidance.

She closed her eyes and silently prayed, asking God to show her how to handle the situation. She asked Him for forgiveness for holding the secret back from her husband—and that her husband would forgive her, also. And she thanked Him for bringing Bobby and Beth into her life.

Only God could give her the answers. Only He could help her.

Feeling much better, she turned away from the window and stared straight ahead. Out of the corner of her eye she saw that Bobby was looking at her, so she turned toward him. He was giving her a strange, probing look.

"What's wrong?" she asked warily,

He shook his head. "I was wondering what you were doing with your eyes closed."

She shrugged. "Just praying."

"About what?"

"That you would forgive me," she said bluntly, staring straight into his eyes.

"I forgive you, then. Isn't that what the Bible tells us to do?" he shot back at her, with no hint of forgiveness in his voice.

"But you don't want to be married to me anymore. Doesn't the Bible say something about that, too?"

"It was never a real marriage, and I don't want to discuss this." He turned away from her hurt expression and looked across the coach. She followed his gaze and noticed that the man across from them was staring at them with interest.

"I say, old man," he began—his accent was that of the British upperclass. "Do you mean you're planning to divorce this woman?"

Bobby scowled. "I don't see how that's any of your business."

"Yes, he is!" Susannah added quickly. "He won't forgive me."

"What did you do, my dear?" he asked sympathetically.

"Susannah!" Bobby scolded.

But she ignored his protest. "I kept a secret from him. But

it was only because I didn't want him to be angry with me. I love him, you see. And I was so afraid that if I told him, he would hate me. So I didn't."

"And he found out anyway, I take it."

"Oh, for goodness sakes, Susannah. Will you—"

"Yes, he did. And now he wants a divorce. But I won't stand for it! Why, my ancestors would positively roll over in their graves if I did such a thing." She took a deep breath and thrust up her chin. "And besides, as I said, I love him. I won't quit until he really forgives me and admits that he loves me, too."

"I never said I loved you," Bobby Joe said. Then he looked chagrined for having allowed himself to be drawn into the conversation. He looked away again.

"But you were *going* to tell me, I *know* you were," she insisted, and then she turned back toward the older man. "You see, he was about to tell me he was in love with me when my father burst into the room and ruined everything."

"A sticky situation indeed," he agreed with a nod. "Allow me to introduce myself to you, by the by! I am Nigel Pemberton, the Earl of Grayston." He bent his head in a regal bow.

Impressed, Susannah smiled at him. "Gracious! A real-life earl? Why, it's a pleasure to make your acquaintance, Lord Grayston. I'm Susannah Butler Aaron, and this is my husband, Bobby Joe Aaron. He owns a large sawmill in Springton, and I'm the town's schoolteacher."

"I hear the lumber business is booming! A pleasure to meet you, sir," Lord Grayston said to Bobby. "And you, Madam. But please, here in America, everyone calls me Nigel. No need to stand on ceremony!"

Bobby gave him a grudging nod and murmured, "Nice to

meet you." He then turned back to the window, bringing his part of the discussion to an end.

Susannah shook her head with a sigh, then looked back at Nigel. "I'm afraid you'll just have to excuse Bobby, Nigel. He's just out of sorts right now."

"Don't blame him atall. I'll wager he'll come around soon enough. I wouldn't lose hope."

"Susannah, please stop talking about me like I'm not here!"

"Well, you're not exactly adding to our conversation, are you? It almost *is* like you're not here!"

"Listen, you can talk about anything else, just quit talking about us. Change the subject, will you?" Bobby demanded.

Susannah felt like crying. She sniffled and dug in her purse for her lace hankie. "But I can't think about anything else! My heart is breaking in two! How can I possibly stop thinking about that?"

"Dear me, Aaron," Nigel inserted. "Why don't you just give over and offer the girl a second chance. She looks like a good, honest sort. I'm sure she won't keep anything from you again."

"Ha!" Bobby said without humor. "She doesn't have an honest bone in her body! It's because of her that my daughter has been kidnapped!"

"The plot does thicken, doesn't it? I say, that is a rather serious charge. How did she cause such a thing to happen?" Nigel leaned forward in his seat, his eyes full of curiosity.

Bobby scowled at him again, so Susannah jumped in. "Well . . .you see, it happened like this. . . ." She proceeded to pour out her story to the man. She normally wouldn't be this forthcoming with a stranger, but she'd felt so alone since Bobby learned her secret, that she had to talk with someone.

Nigel listened intently. After he'd heard it all, he looked

at her with sympathy. "Well, that is a sordid tale, isn't it? But I can see that you didn't mean for things to turn out the way they did!"

"You can?" Susannah asked gratefully. "You see, Bobby? He doesn't think I'm to blame!"

"Now, wait just a moment. I'm not finished. I can readily understand how it is that he blames you."

Susannah's face fell. "You can?"

Bobby snorted. *"Now* somebody's finally making sense!"

"Yes, I do understand, but this is not an unforgivable offense, young man. It was just one mistake. Surely you can see she's sorry and that she loves you," Nigel reasoned.

"This isn't the first secret she's kept from me," Bobby explained grimly. "The first one she kept for years before she finally told me."

"Oh, for goodness sakes, Bobby! I told you I'd promised my sister that I wouldn't tell you."

"Frankly, Susannah, I don't know what to believe. How do I know if you're even telling me the truth about that? You and your father planned to kidnap my daughter! You're not exactly the sort of person that I can trust, are you?" Bobby shook his head wearily, as if he were tiring of the conversation.

"Kidnap?" Nigel exclaimed with raised eyebrows. "You Americans have a strange way of doing things. I'm afraid I'm at sea about this whole ordeal!"

Misunderstanding him, Susannah said, "Nigel, we are not at sea! We're in the middle of Louisiana on a stagecoach! See?" She pointed toward the open window and froze at what she saw.

"No, no, Madam. That is an expression that we use in England. It means. . ."

Susannah interrupted with a shaky voice as she continued to point. "Am. . .am I mistaken? Or is that a band of outlaws riding our way?"

❧

Bobby Joe didn't know why Susannah felt the need to air their family matters to a total stranger. As she chattered away, he'd gone through a range of emotions.

Mostly, although he'd never admit it to his wife, he was amused. He'd never met anyone who could talk like Susannah. The more upset or worried she became, the more she talked.

If only he could believe what she had told him. If only she had just been honest with him from the beginning. *If only, if only. . .* , he thought. There were too many uncertainties where she was concerned. And he knew that it could have all been an elaborate, calculated plan—what he'd been told about his first wife's "secret," the marriage. . .everything. A plan to steal his precious daughter away from him. How could she even pretend to go along with it?

The frightening thing was that Butler could very well sneak his daughter overseas and he'd never get her back. Susannah's mother had practically lived in Paris. If Butler took his daughter there, Bobby didn't know *what* he would do.

But he wouldn't allow himself to think about that. If he did, it would drive him mad.

Despite what Susannah thought of him, he wasn't bitter, and he didn't blame God. He'd done that once before and it had made him miserable. He was determined not to do it again.

And he'd been praying, begging God, really, to allow him to get Beth back. He also prayed that she wouldn't be frightened.

But his thoughts were interrupted in a flash when he realized what Susannah had said.

Outlaws?

Bobby Joe looked out the window and nearly stopped breathing. Five men, their faces covered with bandannas, were riding toward them with guns drawn.

"Get down!" he ordered as he put his arm around Susannah and pulled her down himself.

"Oh, dear!" Nigel murmured up above them. When Bobby Joe realized that the elderly man was frozen in fright, he grabbed him by the front of his shirt and pulled him down, too.

"What. . .what do we. . .do?" Nigel managed, his face a ghostly pale. Bobby hoped the man didn't have a bad heart.

"Just do what they tell us to, all right? Most of the time they just want money and jewelry. Don't fight them—just give them what they want. Nothing is more important than your life," Bobby counseled in a calm voice. Inside, he was anything but calm. He was worried about his wife. While it was true that he didn't trust her or even desire to live with her, he didn't want anything to happen to her, either. Despite everything that had happened, he still loved her. That would take longer to die.

"I can't believe this is happening to me again!" Susannah cried in a hushed voice.

Bobby looked at her, not believing what he was hearing. "What? Do you mean to tell me you've been held up before?"

"Oh my, yes. It was such a silly ordeal, really."

If he lived to be a hundred, he would never understand the woman. *"Silly?"*

She didn't have time to respond before gunshots rang out, causing the coach to grind to a quick halt, dumping all three passengers on the coach floor.

"Oomph!" someone said as they scrambled to right themselves.

"Everyone all right?" Bobby asked as he helped Susannah straighten her dress.

"Yes," they both answered, fear thick in their voices.

Loud voices were shouting back and forth, and then they felt the slight rock of the coach as the driver climbed down from his seat. They were expecting it, but they all jumped when the door was thrown open.

A masked man with frightening gray eyes and a dusty hat pulled down low ordered them to exit the coach. "And don't try being a hero, mister, or you'll end up a dead one," he advised Bobby Joe with a menacing, raspy voice.

Bobby Joe jerked his head in a nod, hoping he wouldn't have to use the gun he'd brought along. Moments earlier, when he'd been on the floor, he'd reached into the saddlebag that he'd brought with them and had removed his pistol. Then he'd slipped it under his coat in the back, tucking it into the waistband of his pants.

Now as they stood outside of the coach, Bobby Joe took a quick inventory of the outlaws. There were five of them in all. The one standing closest had a bag in his hand—probably the money collector. Another by the coach horses had a gun trained on the driver. A third one was untying the luggage from the top of the coach and throwing it down. The other two were still on their horses, their guns aimed at all the captives. The man on the right clearly was the leader. He was barking out the orders for them to hand over all their jewels and money.

He went to Nigel first, and the old man was doing just what Bobby told him to do. He took his ring off and removed the contents of his pockets.

The problems started when they got to Susannah. Bobby Joe should have known that she wouldn't be able to cooperate.

She held out her bag to the man. "Here, this is all you're going to get from me, you mealy-mouthed, slithering varmint! You are certainly *not* going to get my wedding band! I've dealt with your type before, you know, and I am tired of you animals trying to take my things!"

"Susannah!" he hissed. "Would you shut up?"

But she paid him no mind. Apparently she had other ideas. "No, Bobby, I will not shut up! Not when no-accounts like these are trying to terrorize honest folk!"

The man growled, stuck his pistol close to her face, and cocked the gun with a sickening click. "You'd better listen to the man, woman! Shut your trap and give up the goods!" he ordered.

Bobby's heart was beating furiously in his chest. He watched as she looked at the gun closely and then narrowed her eyes as she gazed at the outlaw.

"As I live and breath!" she exclaimed with a surprised laugh that made everyone look at her in astonishment. "If it isn't the Dobbins gang! Weren't you boys arrested and thrown in jail?"

The outlaw's eyes widened with what looked akin to horror, then he knocked his hat back a little to get a better look at Susannah.

"What's the holdup?" the leader barked.

The man who'd been holding the gun on them stomped a boot on the ground, then reached up and took his hat off his head, throwing it down in a fit of temper. He turned and looked at the man on the horse.

"You ain't going to believe it, boss! It's that red-headed woman that got us in all that trouble in Charleston!"

"You're foolin' me," the one on the left exclaimed in disbelief as he and the boss jumped off their horses.

Bobby looked at Susannah. "Susannah, do you *know* these men?"

ten

Susannah nodded, an angry look on her face. "These are the men who tried to rob me years ago! But I had them arrested!"

By now, all the men had stopped what they were doing and had gathered around her. To Bobby, it seemed that she took great pleasure in seeing their discomfort!

"I can't believe it! It *is* her," one of them said in disgust.

The boss narrowed his gaze on her and pointed his gun in her direction. "Because of your never-ending chatter, we spent two years in jail! You 'bout got us hanged!" he charged.

"You *should* have been hanged! How in tarnation did you get out of jail in two years' time? I thought you all were in there for at least thirty years!"

The one standing beside him laughed evilly. "It was no thanks to you! We escaped, you red-headed shrew!"

"Susannah, what is going on here? How exactly did you manage to have these men arrested?" Bobby asked curiously. If he wasn't so scared that they would shoot him, the whole thing would be hilarious.

"I'd like to hear that myself," Nigel piped up.

Susannah folded her arms as she continued to glare at the boss. "You might say I distracted them," she answered evasively.

The outlaw who'd been holding the gun on them spoke up. "Ha! *I'd* say she distracted us, too. Pert' near talked our ears off, is what she did! And while we was trying to get her to shut up, one of the other passengers was able to run off

99

and get the law!"

"We was making perty good money until she messed things up!" another man exclaimed.

To his utter amazement, his wife, the teacher, shook her head in disgust. "We *were*, not we *was!* Didn't any of you boys go to school?"

Sweat was beginning to break out on Bobby's brow. Had the heat of the sun made her delirious? "Susannah!" he hissed again.

Susannah turned to him with a comforting smile and patted him on the arm. "Don't worry, dear. These men aren't going to hurt us. I don't think they have the nerve to shoot us. Why, they had ample opportunity to shoot me last time, and frankly, it would have saved their hide if they had! But they are simply too nice to shoot anybody!" she explained with a carefree shrug.

Feeling helpless to do anything, Bobby looked at the outlaws, whose faces showed more and more anger with everything she said. "Uh. . .please forgive my wife. She's been. . . unwell lately. She doesn't realize what she's saying," he said to the outlaws. Then he grabbed her arm and pulled her closer to him. "Will you stop? You're making them mad."

The boss started laughing, which caused all his fellow outlaws to join in. "She's your wife?" They all laughed. "You have my sympathies!" More laughter.

Bobby felt like he was a player in one of those crazy traveling comedy plays that had come through town a time or two. Nothing was making sense.

Then his wayward wife looked up at him with her big green eyes and whispered, "I'll prove to you they're cowards!"

Then she pulled away from him before he could yank her back. "Quit your laughing and just leave!" she announced, throwing up her hands. "You are not going to get my jewelry or anything else!" She grabbed the bag that held her and Nigel's things and tossed it back to Nigel.

Bobby felt a horrible foreboding as he looked at the leader. He walked over to her and stood so close that she could probably feel him breathing on her. But she didn't moved. The crazy woman just stood there!

Well, he'd finally had enough. He went to grab her again, but the barrel of a gun was poked in his chest, stopping him.

The outlaw holding the gun shook his head. "Despite what she says, I'm not afraid to shoot."

Bobby wasn't willing to chance it. He still had the gun; he just had to figure out a way to use it.

And he prayed that they wouldn't hurt her.

"Is that so?" the boss sneered in Susannah's face. "You expect us to just run along like a pack of cowards?"

"Yes, I do!"

Without warning, the man grabbed Susannah around the waist and threw her over his shoulder.

Bobby Joe sprang into action. He knocked the barrel of the gun in his chest out of his way and ran toward them. Bobby Joe reached them as a shot rang out; he felt himself propelled sideways. Dazed, he could do nothing but stare up at the sky. All he knew was that the side of his head was aching.

Above him he heard Susannah scream, and then his pocket watch was pulled out of the front of his pants and yanked from its chain. He tried to reach up, but he couldn't focus, his head was hurting so badly.

Then all he heard was the sound of horses galloping away and a lot of whoops and hollers from the outlaws.

He closed his eyes as the pain begin to subside. He tried to clear his thoughts.

"Is he dead?" he heard the driver ask.

"No, he's breathing," Nigel answered. "I'm just trying to see how bad the wound is." Bobby felt him probing around the source of his pain, just above his left ear.

He moaned when Nigel hit a sore spot. "It appears to be merely a flesh wound. It grazed his head, but the impact of the bullet knocked him over and stunned him."

"Mr. Aaron! Mr. Aaron, sir, can you hear me?" someone called out above his prone body. He felt someone gently slapping him on the cheeks.

Bobby was finally able to open his eyes, and he was relieved to find out that his vision wasn't as blurry as it had been. "I'm. . .I'm all right. Just help me up."

With the aid of Nigel and the driver, they helped him into a sitting position. "Take it easy. You don't want to pass out," Nigel warned, pressing a handkerchief to his head.

Bobby reached up to take the hankie so that he could see how badly he was bleeding. The rag was covered with blood, but not soaked—a good sign. He pressed it back in place and looked around him.

Then he remembered what had taken place before he'd been shot. "Where's Susannah?" he asked, panic rising in his chest.

"Oh, dear!" Nigel cried as he looked at the driver. "They took her, Mr. Aaron. They didn't take anything else, just her. Rode off into those woods over there, they did!"

"I've got to go after them!" he called out as he jumped to his feet, wincing as a rush of pain jarred his head.

"I don't think you're up to it, old boy. Why don't you rest in the coach while the driver takes us to the nearest town, which is. . . ?"

"Wiseville. There's a doctor by the name of G. T. Wise there who can fix you right up. His brother is the local law.

They'll see to finding your wife," the driver supplied.

But Bobby shook his head. "Nigel, if you can find something to bandage up my head, I'll be able to move better. I'll go looking around in those woods. They're probably camped out somewhere in 'em." He looked at the driver. "Take the coach to Wiseville and let that lawman know what's happened."

"But. . .but this is ludicrous!" Nigel stammered as Bobby stumbled over to the coach. He reached in and pulled out his saddlebags.

"I've got to find her, Nigel. I don't want her hurt!" He pulled out a bandanna and wrapped it around his head, tucking the blood-soaked handkerchief snugly underneath.

"But you're not well, man! You've had a nasty blow to the head! And besides, they have guns!" the earl argued.

"So do I." Bobby reached behind his back and pulled out his pistol.

Nigel sighed. "Well, good luck, sir. Just try to keep from being shot again, will you?"

Bobby smiled grimly, then winced when that action sent a jolt of pain through his head. "Thank you," he managed.

He started off toward the woods, each footfall jarring his wound. But he was determined to ignore the pain and find his wife.

His *wife*. No matter what she'd done to him, no matter how badly she had deceived him, he still thought of her as his wife.

He should be planning how he would ring her neck when he got her back, but he couldn't. All he could think of was holding her close in his arms and never letting her go.

But of course, he would let her go. There was no future for them. When they arrived in Charleston, he would leave her at her father's home.

That would be that.

That thought should have made him happy, but it didn't. It only made him feel sorry. Sorry that she'd lied to him. Sorry that he couldn't forgive her.

He knew the Scriptures. He knew that Jesus had asked his followers to forgive seventy times seven times. He'd done things in the past himself that others had forgiven *him* for. But every time he thought about her scheming to take his daughter away from him, his anger would renew itself.

He prayed as he walked and searched for a trail. He prayed that God would forgive him for his unforgiveness. But most of all, he prayed that Susannah would be unharmed and safe—and that God would lead him to the gang.

He would never forgive himself if he failed to find her.

❧

Susannah sat on the dirty ground as Durwood Dobbins, one of the three brothers for whom the gang was named, tried to make a fire. The other brothers were Dugin, the boss, and Dustin, the youngest of the three. The other two outlaws—Bodin and Butch—were friends of the brothers. She didn't know their last names, but did know that the two of them also were brothers.

All of the gang had a rough, unkempt appearance. Their hair was short, but it looked as if they'd cut it themselves—with a dull knife! Their teeth were yellow, and they had the foulest breath she'd ever had the misfortune of experiencing. Their clothes were filthy, and the way they scratched, they must have been crawling with fleas.

They had led her to the camp, which was a short walk from where the holdup took place. Pushing her to the ground, they'd tied her hands in front of her with an old rope. Apparently they were inept at tying a rope; five minutes after they'd snugged the knot up tight, her hands were free. She kept them folded down in her skirts, pretending she was still tied.

Of course, all of this was done while she cried. She just couldn't seem to help it. And she wasn't a quiet, gentle crier, either. Oh no! She'd always had the nasty habit of wailing loudly.

Right now she felt as though she would cry forever. They'd killed her husband. And she let them know she wasn't happy about it. . .all the way to the camp.

She bellowed that they'd taken away the love of her life and that they'd murdered a father, leaving his only child an orphan. She blasted them for finally becoming tough outlaws, when always before they'd merely been blustering cowards. Why did they have to begin their murderous ways today, with her husband?

Only Durwood was with her now. All the rest had disappeared into the woods.

"How could you?" she wailed. "How could you murder my husband? He was only trying to *help* me!" She gave up the pretense of being tied up and covered her face with her hands.

"Awww, I ain't the one who shot 'im!" Durwood whined. "It was Butch that done it. And I was sure it only grazed 'im anyway." He reached over and pulled her hands off her face and wound the rope back around them. "Now quit your cater-wallin' and boo-hooing! You're givin' me a headache!"

"No, I won't quit crying, and it's just too bad that you're getting a headache," she threw back at him in a quavering holler as she easily untied the rope. "I'm a widow, thanks to you!"

Durwood held his head between his hands, a pained expression on his face. "I've *had* it! Just sit still while I go and find somethin' to gag you with!"

Tears continued to fall as she watched Durwood disappear into the woods. She looked back at the firewood and noticed that he hadn't even managed to start the fire.

These men are so inept, she thought, as she slipped her husband's pocket watch—which she'd carefully removed from Durwood's pocket—into her own pocket.

But even in the midst of her hysterics she realized an opportunity when she saw one. After wiping her eyes, she pulled herself up and began walking away from the camp, retracing the path through the woods that the outlaws had followed when they had brought her to their camp.

She'd walked only about a yard or so when a man appeared from behind a group of trees.

To her utter amazement, it was Bobby Joe with a bandanna tied around his head.

"You're not dead!" she squealed as she started to run toward him.

"Susannah. . . ," she heard him whisper, his voice full of happy relief. He began running toward her.

He grabbed her up in his strong embrace, whirling her around in jubilation.

"Oh, honey, I thought I'd lost you. I don't know what I would have done if. . ." He shook his head as he put her down and stared at her intensely. Then he pulled her close and kissed her. It was a desperate kiss. A kiss filled with relief that he'd found her alive and joy that he had her once again.

She also sensed his love mixed as she felt his hands smooth her hair, and his lips softly caress her own, then trail off to leave tiny kisses all about her face.

He loved her! She could feel it in her heart. Maybe he had forgiven her. Maybe he wouldn't be angry with her anymore.

Then he pulled back, and she looked up into his eyes once more.

Boy, had she ever been wrong!

eleven

Gone was his look of relief and love. Back was his scowl and flashing eyes. His hands tightened on her arms.

"How could you act so recklessly? Don't you know you could've gotten us all killed?" he yelled, giving her a shake.

"I didn't mean to! I was just. . ."

"Having a bout of insanity?" he finished for her.

Susannah frowned. "Would you stop shaking me? I feel like my brain's rattling around in my poor ol' head!"

He let go of her, then said with a sneer, "You mean you have one?"

"Oh, now you're just being nasty, and to tell you the truth, I've had enough nastiness from those heathen outlaws!" They glared at each other for an angry moment, then Susannah's gaze drifted up to the bandanna.

"Oh, Bobby, I'm so sorry. I haven't even asked how your head is. I was devastated when I thought that they'd killed you." She reached up and touched just under the makeshift bandage.

He stood still as she examined him. "It dazed me for a bit, but it only nicked me. Has it stopped bleeding?"

She lifted the bandage and nodded. "Yes, but you really need to wash it and clean it up."

"Uh. . .Susannah? Just where are the outlaws now? How did you get away from them?" he asked, looking around.

She shrugged. "They got tired of hearing me cry and carry on, at least that's what they said. Anyway, they tied me up and left. But they couldn't tie a little old knot to save their lives, because I quickly got loose. . .twice as a matter of fact!" she said proudly.

"Oh! Here's your pocket watch." She handed him the watch, but he didn't say anything as he looked at it. He hadn't been expecting it, she guessed.

"I doubt they realize I'm gone. Why, I've never seen a bunch of men who so badly need to consider another occupation!" She fussed with redoing her ponytail and missed the look that fell across Bobby's features.

"Well, they know now," he said flatly.

"What?"

"I said, they know you escaped them."

She flipped her long ponytail back, glad to have it off her neck once more. "How do you know that?"

"Because they're standing right behind you."

With a quick intake of breath, she whirled around to face all five of the men. Bobby pulled her behind him. It was then that she noticed the gun in his hand. Where had that come from?

"There's no need for that, mister. We're giving her back," Dugan, the boss outlaw, told them wearily.

"That's right," Bodin chimed in. "She ain't nothing but a tiresome chatterbox. Give us all headaches, she did." He rubbed his dirty forehead to prove the point.

Susannah was becoming miffed as they went on and on about how they couldn't be around her one more minute.

She came out from behind Bobby, her hands on her hips, and snapped, "How can you let them talk about me like that? You have a gun. Shoot them!"

Bobby looked at her and began to chuckle. "I haven't heard anything I disagreed with yet!"

"You, Bobby Joe Aaron, can just stay here with them then! I'm leaving!" With that she turned and stalked into the woods.

Still chuckling, Bobby slowly backed away from the outlaws, his gun pointed toward them, until he reached the trees. He then ran to catch her. Taking her by the arm, he refused to let go of it, even when she tried to jerk it away from him.

"Now, don't put up a fuss, honey. I'm sure that's not the first time someone's told you that you talk too much. You should be happy—that's what saved your life!"

She rolled her eyes and looked away from him. "At least I did *something* right," she answered with a sniff.

"I didn't even have to use my gun."

She whirled around and glared at him. "I can't believe it. You had a gun and you didn't shoot those varmints when they were carrying me off?"

"If you'll remember, Miss I'll-Prove-They're-Not-So-Tough, I was lying on the ground with a gunshot wound to the head!"

"Oh, yeah," she said with a frown. "Then why didn't you use it before they started robbing us? Or how about now? You're just going to let those outlaws go scot-free?"

He looked at her as one would a child. "Susannah, I was expecting to just give them the money they wanted and let them leave, remember? I was only going to use it if they got rough. Well, they only got rough because you wouldn't stop giving them a hard time! By then, it was too late! They shot me!" His voice had escalated to a yell.

"Well, goodness gracious! You don't have to scream at me!"

He took a deep breath and continued, more calmly, "And I didn't try to capture them just now because, if you haven't noticed, we are slightly outnumbered. I would be crazy to try to bring them in by myself, especially with this headache I've got. And besides, Nigel and the driver are on their way to get the sheriff. They'll take care of them soon enough."

He took her arm and gave her a gentle pull so that they would resume walking. "And besides, men don't scream. We yell. There's a difference."

As much as Susannah wanted to, she wisely chose not to comment on that observation and allowed him to lead them through the woods.

They'd walked some twenty minutes before he stopped and looked around carefully. "We should have been out of the woods by now. We must have headed off in the wrong direction."

She looked at Bobby and noticed that his face was pale; sweat was beading on his forehead and temple. "Bobby, are you all right? Head hurting terribly?"

He shook his head, but she noticed that he winced when he did so. "I'm all right. It's just a little hot out here."

"Actually, it's chilly." She led him to a tree stump. "Here, sit down and let me check that wound."

"All right. I could use a rest." He sat down and closed his eyes for a moment.

As Susannah checked his wound, she began to worry. He didn't look well, and she thought his words were beginning to slur. After inspecting the wound, she knew it needed to be cleaned. It would become infected if it wasn't attended to soon.

"Bobby, I'm going for help. You just stay here, and I'll be back as soon as I can," she told him, her hand resting on his back.

When she started to walk away, he put a hand on her arm, stopping her. "No. You'll just get lost," he told her, his voice weak.

She bent down, holding his hand up to her cheek. "Bobby, we're already lost. And if you walk anymore, you could pass out! You don't look well."

Still, he managed to stand up. "I can make it."

She shook her head in exasperation. "I give up! You're just too stubborn to argue with. Put your arm around me and lean on me." She wound his arm around her shoulders.

After thirty minutes, they hadn't managed to get very far. Bobby was leaning more and more on her, until she was sure she was taking most of his weight. And boy, was he heavy!

She was just about to suggest that they sit a spell, when they came upon a homestead. There were scads of children running around playing, and with them was a mixture of chickens, dogs, cats, and even a couple of tamed squirrels. It was a strange group, but they all seemed to get along—including the animals.

Then out of the house came a heavyset woman wearing a large white apron. Her brown hair was combed up into a bun and her round face was smiling merrily. The chaos didn't seem to bother her. She just walked out into the middle of it and sat on a bench. Her children were quick to gather around her.

"Now then, children. I'm a-hoping by all the laughing and carrying on that you've all finished your chores!" she said with a mock stern expression; her brown eyes were twinkling.

"Yessum!" they all cried in unison.

"I fed the chickens all on my lonesome!" a little one boasted, her dirty face surrounded by a mop of brown curls.

"It's true, Ma! I see'd her with my own two eyes!"

"You saw her, Malcolm," she corrected.

"Yessum. That's what I said!"

The woman shook her head, laughing.

Susannah was about to drop from Bobby's weight. She walked closer, hoping that this woman was as friendly to strangers as she was to her children. With isolated country people, though, you never knew.

They walked into the clearing in full view of the woman and her children. Suddenly the dog started barking, which made the chickens squawk. The family all turned and looked at them, their eyes curious but wary.

"Look, Ma! Strangers!" one of the kids called out.

"I'm so sorry to impose on you, Ma'am. But we were set upon by outlaws and my husband was hurt," Susannah explained as they walked closer.

The woman studied them for a second longer, then seemed satisfied that they weren't dangerous. She jumped up and walked hurriedly to them. "You poor, poor folks! I heard that there were outlaws about in these parts." She took Bobby's other arm and put it around her own shoulders, taking some of the weight off of Susannah.

"Let's get him into the house. Then we'll see to that wound."

Susannah thanked her gratefully, then looked at Bobby with growing concern. He was aware of what was going on, but he seemed too tired to speak.

In no time they had him inside the house, and they helped him onto one of the many beds that stood in a large room.

"I'm Ruby Davis, by the way," the woman told Susannah as she worked at removing the bandage from Bobby's head. "My husband, Thomas, is out tilling soil to prepare for our crops, just beyond the trees out back. He and his brother share the land and the profits. The children out front are all mine."

Susannah shared a smile with Mrs. Davis. "You have your hands full!"

"Yes, I do at that! But I enjoy it. I've always enjoyed children. Of course, I never thought I'd have so many, but that was what the good Lord gave me, and I've never been happier."

She made a tsk-tsk noise as she looked at the wound. "We've got to get that cleaned out. But I think he'll be all right. The blow to his head is probably what hurt him the most. I'll bet there's swelling inside his head." She busied herself getting a bowl of clean hot water and a soft cloth and began to wash the wound.

"We'll need to wake him every hour or so to make sure he's alert."

Susannah shook her head, amazed at what the woman was saying. "How do you know so much?"

"I have nine kids! Believe me, they've been through more illnesses and accidents than you could imagine. You learn through experience!"

Mrs. Davis fixed him up with a proper bandage and then fed them both a vegetable broth that she'd made. Within an hour, Bobby had perked up and seemed to be less tired. He had dozed a little after eating, but after twenty minutes or so, he awoke on his own.

"Well, you look a sight better, Mr. Aaron! How are you feelin'?" Mrs. Davis asked, helping Susannah prop him up with a couple of pillows.

Bobby touched the side of his head where the bandage was. "I've still got a slight headache, but I'm feeling a lot better." He looked at Susannah and actually smiled at her.

But Susannah wasn't going to hope that it meant anything. She'd learned the hard way not to do that with Bobby.

"Hey there," she said as she felt his cool forehead. "How's my hero?"

He shook his head. "Hero? It wasn't me who rescued you. You drove those outlaws crazy by. . ."

Her mouth gaped open. "Oh, now, Bobby, don't go bringing that up again!"

He took her hand and planted a kiss on her palm. It absolutely took her breath away, but she struggled to pretend it didn't. "I'm just kidding, Red. Really, I appreciate you looking after me. I know it wasn't easy."

She swallowed and tried to be nonchalant. "Oh, it's what any wife would do." She shrugged and looked at him, and she saw that he was giving her a knowing look, as if he wasn't fooled by her act.

At that point Mrs. Davis excused herself to look after her children and left the room. As soon as she was gone, Bobby started to get out of bed.

"Just what do you think you're doing?" Susannah scolded, trying to hold him down.

"Susannah, have you forgotten what we've set out to do? We've got to go so we can catch up with your father."

"But. . .but your head!"

"It's fine. Honestly, Susannah, I feel okay. We have to keep going."

They looked at one another for a moment, and Susannah read the determination in his eyes. Sighing, she threw up her hands. "Oh, all right. But don't blame me if you end up passing out!"

He picked up his saddlebag from the floor and then, with Susannah holding his hand, walked into the living-dining area of the roomy yet plain house.

All the children were seated on benches at the long oak table, and Mrs. Davis was serving them their dinner. Bobby Joe started to tell her that they were leaving, when the door to the house burst open and a big, burly man walked in, a spray of rain sweeping in behind him. He was soaking wet from the top of his blond, shaggy head to the soles of his large leather work boots.

"It's raining hard out there," he exclaimed as he hung his hat on the tree beside the door. "There won't be any plowing done today!"

Just then he noticed Susannah and Bobby. His eyebrows shot up in surprise. "We've got company, Mama?"

Mrs. Davis smiled as she rushed over to him with a cloth so he could dry himself. "We sure do, Thomas. These poor folks, Mr. and Mrs. Aaron, were held up by a gang of robbers. And Mr. Aaron here was shot. I just bandaged him up a bit."

Susannah and Bobby greeted the good-natured man, but then Bobby said, "Thank you, Mrs. Davis, for your help, but we need to be going. We were on our way to collect my daughter, and I don't want to be late." It wasn't the whole truth, but close enough that they wouldn't have to explain, Susannah supposed.

Thomas laughed and shook his head. "You won't be leaving today and probably not tomorrow. That storm is a bad one, and it shows signs of lasting!"

twelve

Bobby Joe could see that Thomas Davis had been right. The rain and wind were now treacherous, the storm too bad for them to go anywhere.

But they were in a dilemma. Bobby Joe had planned for them to find Nigel and the driver of the coach and then continue on their way. Now, they'd have to wait and take another coach. It frustrated him, but there was nothing to do but wait.

So he accepted the Davises' invitation to stay with them until the storm blew over. Bobby Joe and Susannah sat down and ate dinner with the family, since all they'd had to eat was the broth Mrs. Davis had served them earlier.

Susannah, he noticed, kept looking at him, a worried expression on her face. He tried to reassure her that he was all right, but to no avail.

Actually, it felt good to have someone worry over him. He'd been taking care of himself for years, so it was a nice change.

He didn't understand her at all. Why had she been in tears when he'd found her? She had fallen into his arms and had held on to him as if she never wanted to let go. And it wasn't just that she was glad to see someone she knew—she'd clearly been relieved that he was okay. She said that she thought he'd been killed. And she'd cried her heart out over it, according to the gang.

It just didn't add up. How could a woman who seemed to care so much about him lie to him and deceive him so readily?

Maybe she'd been telling the truth. Maybe she'd never

intended to take Beth away from him. Maybe she *had* only pretended to appease her father.

His head began to pound, and he realized that he was thinking too hard. He'd just have to wait and see how things turned out. If this was indeed the real Susannah and she really did love him. . .well then, he'd have to rethink things. Until then, he'd watch. And wait.

After dinner, the Davises invited them to sit with them and have a cup of coffee. The children busied themselves in the large room with checkers and simple wooden toys, and a couple of the older girls took out their sewing and knitting. One of the older boys, who looked to be twelve or thirteen, was busy trying to carve something out of a piece of wood.

The Davis house was one story tall and sturdy, with an open hallway running through its middle. It was a large structure, but it had few rooms. The kitchen was off to one side, with a large pantry adjoining it. There was a small table there, which primarily was used by the girls during the day for play or to do their studies. On the other side of the hall was the dining room-living room area, as well as two bedrooms. One was the large room that contained four double beds and one baby bed. All of the children doubled up in the beds to sleep in the room together. Mr. and Mrs. Davis's bedroom looked smaller.

It wasn't a fancy dwelling like his own house, Bobby thought, but it seemed more like a real home somehow. More comfortable and welcoming.

He watched Susannah sip her coffee and talk with Mrs. Davis; she seemed to fit into this family setting as if she were made for it. He could imagine her being surrounded by many children, happy and loving.

His children.

His heart skipped a beat as that thought entered his head.

He didn't question it, though, he just accepted it and thought on it some more. Maybe he'd known all along that he would fall in love with her—that he'd want her to bear his children, to love him, to care for him, to grow old with him.

He hated feeling unsure about her, hated the feeling of mistrust that took hold of him whenever she smiled at him.

He also knew that the vows he'd taken were sacred ones. He'd renewed his relationship with God, and he knew that God wouldn't approve of a divorce. And he wasn't planning to try to get one.

Brother Caleb, his pastor, had told him many times that God could make a way where there seemed to be no way. He needed God's wisdom and guidance now. He wanted God to show him the truth. He wanted God to restore to him the family that he so desperately wanted.

Somehow he wasn't as worried about his daughter. Once he had calmed down, he'd realized that Butler wouldn't harm his little girl. He just didn't want Beth to be frightened.

But God would keep her safe and give her peace. He'd prayed that the moment he'd realized that Butler had taken her, and he knew that God had heard his prayer.

He had been staring at Susannah when he'd become lost in his thoughts. When she looked back at him, his mind focused on her.

She looked at him with such concern and love that it made his heart swell nearly out of his chest. Even after all he'd said to her, she still could look at him that way. Amazing.

He smiled at her over the rim of his cup to assure her that he was doing fine. She smiled back with a relieved smile, then looked back at Mrs. Davis.

"You love her a lot, don't ya," Mr. Davis commented softly from his chair beside Bobby Joe.

Bobby Joe looked at him with surprise. "Beg your pardon?"

"I was just commenting on how much you seem to love Mrs. Aaron there. Oh, don't be embarrassed by it. I've had the same look on my face now for nigh unto eighteen years. I ought to recognize it when I see it on someone else!"

Bobby smiled sheepishly. "I didn't realize I was so transparent. I didn't used to be."

"Aw, love'll do that to ya. Makes us all act a little silly, I guess," Thomas Davis continued before taking a sip of his coffee.

"I guess you're right about that. I don't know what makes me sillier or crazier—love or Susannah. I've never met another woman like her." He shook his head, showing his confusion.

Thomas laughed softly. "I understand what you're sayin'! Thought that a time or two about the missus." He reached over and picked up a marble that had rolled over by his chair and tossed it back to his boys. "Where do you two hail from?"

"Springton, Texas. My brothers and I own a sawmill, and Susannah is the town's schoolteacher."

"Well, I'm sure that my wife and yours will have plenty in common, then. She was schooled in the finest boarding schools and got a good education. She teaches our children since the school is too far from here." He took another sip of coffee. "Ruby was from a wealthy family in Shreveport, but gave all that up and decided to marry me. Her family disinherited her, but she wouldn't be swayed. When I told her that I'd probably never be rich, she said 'good'! She told me that being rich and living without love had made her nothing but miserable; so being poor, with love, had to be better."

Bobby Joe laughed. "Well, she's the happiest woman I believe I've ever seen!"

Thomas agreed with him, while looking at Bobby Joe

keenly. "All it takes is trust in the Lord and lots of love. If you both serve the Lord with all your heart, then your marriage will always be strong because you'll treat each other with the same love that God gives to us. It's simple, really," he finished with the wisdom that only comes with experience.

Bobby Joe thought about that and realized that he was right. He'd lived his life without God for too many years, and it had brought him nothing but misery. Since he'd given God another chance, he'd felt himself begin to change. And even though he was in the middle of a crisis, he still could feel a peace within his heart.

God could change things.

He looked again at his wife and caught her eye once more. He might not know yet that he could trust her, but he did know one thing—he *wasn't* going to leave her in Charleston.

❧

"My, you and your husband make the handsomest couple. Have you been married long?" Ruby Davis asked as she and Susannah sat a little ways away from the men, sipping their coffee.

"Actually, we've only been married for three weeks," Susannah answered, not really wanting to get into the business of her marriage.

"Three weeks!" Mrs. Davis squealed in delight. "Why, Thomas! Do you know that these two are newlyweds? Isn't that something?"

"Well, congratulations!" Thomas told them both.

"Well, I'm confused, though," Mrs. Davis inserted. "I thought I heard you say you were going after your daughter, Mr. Aaron."

Bobby nodded. "That's right. I was a widower before I married Susannah," he explained, saying as little as possible.

Blessedly, the Davises let the subject drop after that, and soon everyone was getting ready for bed. Susannah watched as they tucked all their children into bed, praying with each one, then giving them all a goodnight kiss.

Susannah's heart ached to be part of a family like this one. A family that was full of love and happiness.

She walked over to where Ruby had set out two pallets in front of the fireplace for her and Bobby Joe. She felt self-conscious in the oversize flannel gown that Ruby had lent her, as she sat on her pallet next to Bobby.

He was staring into the fire, but turned to smile at her when he felt her presence.

"This is quite a family, isn't it?" Susannah commented as she turned to lie down under her covers. "I don't believe I've ever seen a nicer one!"

Bobby did the same on his pallet and turned to face her with his hand propping up his head. "I think so, too. They don't have a lot of money, but it doesn't seem to matter."

Susannah nodded as she looked at him in the firelight. "I wish I'd had a family like this one growing up," she admitted, her voice wistful.

Bobby's eyebrow rose. "Are you saying that the Butlers of Charleston fell short of the goal of being a model family? I thought you people were the cream of the crop?"

Susannah glared at him. "You didn't exactly grow up poor, Bobby. You Aarons have the biggest house in the county!"

"I know, Red. Don't get all angry at me. I didn't mean to be sarcastic." He reached out and tugged on a lock of her wavy hair. "Tell me what your family was like."

He was calling her "Red" again, she realized. Happiness and contentment flooded her heart at his sentiment, and she forgot all about being mad at him. "My mother was never at home, and my father ordered us around like we were little soldiers in his army," she said matter-of-factly. "But you probably already know this. I'm sure Leanna told you."

He shook his head. "Actually, she would never talk about her childhood, other than stories of the two of you. She loved to talk about the good times you two had together."

Susannah smiled, remembering how wonderful her elder sister had been to her. "She was more a mother to me than our own mother had been. She always looked after me."

Bobby's eyes seemed to melt into her own. "I'm sorry, Red. Every little girl should have a happy home."

"That's why I never would have taken Beth to my father, Bobby. Why would I want to do that to her, knowing what kind of life she would have if I succeeded?" she implored, willing him to understand.

For a moment Bobby looked away, toward the fire. Then she heard him say, "I believe you."

"You what?" Susannah was afraid to breathe, fearing that she would miss the answer.

He looked at her. "I said that I believe you."

"You do?"

"I just said I did."

"Oh, yeah. . ." Her voice drifted off as she realized how dimwitted she must sound. But she was so dumbfounded. . . .

"Can I ask you one thing, though?"

She tucked her hair back behind her ear in a nervous gesture and cleared her throat. "Okay."

"Why did you come to Springton if you had no intention of taking Beth?"

"I wanted to teach," she answered simply.

Bobby looked confused. "Then why didn't you just take a teaching job in Charleston?"

"Daddy wouldn't allow it."

Suddenly Bobby's eyes widened as if he was beginning to understand. "And he used the teaching job as a lure to get you out here," he guessed correctly.

"Yes, that's about it."

Letting out a breath of disgust, he fell back on his pillow. "That devious old coot!"

The statement didn't require an answer, so she followed suit and laid back on her pillow.

Susannah thought about everything that he'd told her, and she wondered again about what it all meant where she was concerned. She knew that even if he still planned to leave her in Charleston, she wouldn't stay there.

But she couldn't make him love her. She couldn't make him take her back.

She lay there for probably half an hour and thought and thought about it, until she could think no more. She was never going to get any sleep unless she knew the answer to her question.

"Bobby!" she whispered, turning her head toward him. His eyes opened slowly, and he looked at her. "Are you asleep?"

He blinked and rubbed his eyes. "Well, I'm not anymore."

"Oh. Sorry to wake you. But I really need to ask you something."

He groaned and turned over to his side. "Can't you wait until morning? I think I've done my share of talking today. . .and so have you," he grumbled.

"Oh, pooh! It's just one itsy-bitsy little old question, Bobby Joe Aaron. Surely you have enough words left to answer it!"

"Okay, okay!" he answered, putting a hand to his head as if all the talking was hurting it. "Just ask, so I can get back to sleep."

"I want to know if you still plan to leave me in Charleston," she blurted out, her words leaving her mouth as quickly as she could get them out.

"No. Now let's get some sleep." He flipped back on his back and closed his eyes.

"Did. . .did you say no?" she asked, reaching over to give him a shake. "Bobby! Did you say no?"

"Susannah! You said you only had one question, not three, now sleep."

"Bobby!" she cried in a loud whisper.

"Yes, yes—I said no!"

"Oh! Well. . .thank you." She laid back down with her hand over her heart. She could feel it pounding through the covers.

Suddenly she felt him touch her other hand and take it in his own.

Okay, she thought. *He isn't going to leave me in Charleston, but does that mean he wants to stay married to me?*

She wanted to ask, but she didn't dare. It was enough that he would take her back with him.

For now it was enough.

"Goodnight, Red," he whispered sleepily, his eyes already closed.

She stared at his strong profile in the firelight and returned his grip. "Goodnight, Bobby."

It was enough.

thirteen

The rain was still coming down the next morning when Susannah awoke. She found the sound of the steady rain on the roof soothing, and there was a fresh scent in the air, since their fire had long ago burned out.

Rubbing her eyes, she slowly turned toward Bobby's sleeping pallet and found it empty. She pulled herself up slowly, cringing when her muscles refused to do what she wanted them to do. The floor hadn't been the most comfortable place to sleep!

But it hadn't bothered her at all while she slept, because she had dreamed the most wonderful dreams. Most of them involved Bobby and herself. In one, they were on a picnic, and Bobby was picking her flowers to put in her hair. In another, it was Christmas and Beth was with them as they unwrapped their presents while sitting by the tree. Bobby had unwrapped his present pulling out a hand-knitted sweater that she'd painstakingly made for him. He'd reached over and had given her a gentle kiss on the lips. What was so strange about this was that Susannah couldn't knit! But all the same, she'd felt such a feeling of contentment and happiness. Much like she imagined that the Davises must feel. Much like she wanted to experience in real life.

Shaking herself from her musings, she looked about the large room, listening to see if anyone else had awakened. The light was dim, but she had no idea what time it was because she knew the weather would have darkened the sky.

She could hear sounds coming from across the open hallway, and she figured that they'd all gone over to the kitchen.

Sighing, she crawled out from under the covers. Then, wrapping the blanket around her shoulders, she walked outside, steeling herself for the trek she needed to make to the outhouse.

Taking a deep breath, she covered her head with the blanket and ran down the steps of the house, into the backyard. Rain pelted her as she ran to the little wooden building that sat too far from the house, as far as Susannah was concerned!

She ran under the tiny overhang that did little to keep the rain from hitting her and pulled at the handle. It appeared to be either stuck or locked. Knocking, she called out to see if anyone was in there.

A high-pitched child's voice called out that Rupert was occupying the outhouse at the moment.

Well, little Rupert took his time, but finally he opened the door. And just as he skipped away, he sang out, "Be careful of Freddie!"

Susannah sighed in frustration, thinking "Freddie" was another one of the Davis children. But when she stuck her head in, she saw that the interior was empty. Shrugging, she went on in and shut the door.

But the mystery of Freddie didn't take long to reveal itself. Just as she was about to exit the outhouse, "Freddie" met her face to face.

A scream escaped before she quickly squelched it with a hand over her mouth. Horrified, she cautiously took a few steps backward, until she had no more room to move.

Above the door was a ledge, and lying on that ledge and hanging down from it in front of the door was the most massive snake Susannah had ever seen. Actually, it was the first

.snake she'd ever seen, but it most certainly had to be abnormally large!

Praying for a window was futile, since she knew that the only openings were a few holes cut high on the door and the sides of the building for air.

She stood frozen, watching in horror as the snake moved this way and that, looking at her with much too much interest.

After a moment she realized that she had to get her thoughts together and find a way out. She wished she knew more about snakes; she had no idea how to identify them by species.

She remembered a story that Rachel Stone had told her about a snake that almost bit her daughter. Her husband had shot and killed it before it could strike, but she'd said the snake had been a venomous one.

Oh, what kind was it? she struggled to remember. *A rattler! That's what she'd called it, because it had a tail that rattled.*

Well, she hadn't heard a rattle, at least not yet, from this one. Carefully she stood on her tiptoes and looked at its body.

No rattle.

Her relief only lasted a moment before she realized that it could well be one of the other varieties of deadly snakes that lived in these parts. She'd heard the boys in her class talk about them, so she knew they existed. This particular snake was dark colored and had three pale strips running down its back. Was that good or bad? She just didn't know.

Maybe she could distract it! If she could get it to slide over, she could make a run for it!

She said a quick prayer under her breath, then scooted over, away from the door. The beady eyes followed her, the evil-looking tongue darting at her as if the animal were making fun of her.

"Uh. . .here snakey, snakey," she called, feeling silly. Just how did one call a snake, anyway? "Come here, boy. . .or girl. . .whatever you are." But the snake just hung there in its spot, looking at her.

Feeling desperate, she held up her arm, trying to get the snake's attention. Well, this got its attention, all right. It moved its head toward her hand, nearly bumping into it.

With a squeal, she pulled back her hand. The snake went back to where it had been before.

At least it hadn't bitten her, she thought, though that brought little comfort. It didn't mean that it *couldn't* bite her if it wanted to.

The thing was, she just didn't have the nerve to chance it.

So she slowly sank to the wood-plank floor and pulled her knees up to her chin, where she was as far from the snake as she could possibly be.

She would just have to wait for help.

❧

Bobby Joe had searched the whole house twice over and still had not found his wife. Where in the world had she gone? It was raining too hard for her to want to go for a walk, and he'd just been out at the barn and knew she wasn't there. It just didn't make sense. He reached up to scratch his head, but when he encountered the bandage, he grimaced and lowered his hand. He needed to do something about taking that bandage off!

He went back into the kitchen, where all the Davis kids and their parents were preparing breakfast. That, too, seemed to be a family affair.

"I can't find Susannah anywhere! I just don't understand where she's run off to!"

Ruby wiped her hands on her apron and shook her head. "Goodness me! I can't imagine where she might be!" She looked at her children. "Have any of you seen Mrs. Aaron?"

They all shook their heads.

Bobby Joe scratched his head in bewilderment. "I guess I'll go see if she's outside." He started to leave, but then he felt a tug on his pant leg.

"She's with Freddie," he told him, looking up at him with big hazel-green eyes.

"Excuse me? Did you say she's with someone named Freddie?"

"Yep!" he answered, then walked away.

"Wait, uh. . ." He looked at Ruby. "What's his name?" He pointed to the little boy, who was now trying to take a fried potato from the counter.

"Oh, that one's little Rupert."

"He said something about Susannah being with Freddie. . .?"

Ruby's eyes widened. "Freddie? Oh, dear!" she exclaimed, putting a hand over her mouth. Laughter was gleaming from her eyes.

Bobby Joe's concern was fading and jealousy was rearing its ugly head. "Just who is Freddie?" he demanded, putting his hands on his hips.

"Oh, now, don't get your back up! Freddie is a garter snake that sometimes visits the outhouse. I think if you go outside, you'll find her there. Poor dear is probably scared to death."

His hands fell back to his sides. "A snake?" he asked, dumbfounded. "Rupert, did you see Susannah go into the outhouse?"

The child nodded. "Yessir," he said, his mouth full of fried potato. He reached for another piece, but got his hand slapped for the effort.

Bemused, Bobby turned toward the door. "Then I guess I'd better go and fetch her!"

"Why don't a few of you go with him to round up that snake," Ruby ordered.

Not a few, but the whole horde of Davis children followed him out to the outhouse. They squealed when the rain began to hit them, but soon they were enjoying it.

Bobby tried the door, but found it locked. "Susannah? Are you in there?"

From inside the building he heard a frightened voice call out, "Bobby? Is that you?"

Trying to control the laughter bubbling up within his chest, he answered, "Yes, it's me. You need to unlock the door."

"I can't! Bobby, there's a snake in here, and I'm afraid it'll bite me!"

"It's just a garter snake, Red. It's not going to bite you. Now, hurry! I'm getting soaked!"

"Are you sure?"

That question brought a round of giggles from the children, who were listening as they splashed around him. He had to chuckle himself.

"Yes, I'm sure. Trust me."

From inside he heard a shuffling around. Then he heard her talking as if she were speaking to a scared child. "All right, snakey. I'm just going to reach around you and unlock this little old door, all right? Now, don't look at me like that, snakey, because my little old heart just can't take it. That's a good boy. There, there. . .Eek!" he heard her squeal.

"Susannah? What's wrong?" Bobby called out.

"It touched me! Eeeew! Yuk! It was horrible."

Bobby was soaked from head to toe, but it was worth it just to hear her carry on.

"He's not. . .going. . .to hurt you. Open. . .the door!" he said between chuckles.

"Bobby Joe Aaron, are you laughing at me?" she asked, clearly outraged.

"Uh. . .sort of."

The door flew open, and she walked carefully around the hanging snake. Just when she was almost home free, it swung up and touched her nose. It was enough to send her screaming out of the building and into Bobby Joe's arms.

Bobby Joe held her, but he couldn't prevent himself from laughing.

When she realized this, she flung herself from his arms and began to pelt his chest with her fists, not even noticing that her blanket had fallen to the ground. "Will you quit laughing? I was scared out of my wits!"

He caught her hands. "I'm sorry, Susannah, but you've got to admit it was funny."

She jerked her hands loose and backed away, glaring at him. "I see nothing funny about it! And I think it's highly ungentlemanly of you to say it is! I thought it was a poisonous snake, you fiend. I could have died!"

"Oh, Red. Garter snakes won't kill you," he tried to placate, as he brushed a lock of wet hair from her forehead.

Obviously that wasn't the right thing to say. "I didn't know it was a garter snake, Mr. Smartypants! If I did, I wouldn't have stayed in there!"

"Of course you wouldn't have," he said, biting his lip to keep from laughing.

"You don't believe me!" She shook her head in exasperation. "Well, you just believe what you want! I don't have another thing to say to you!" And with that she sniffed, picked the blanket up off the ground, then thrust her nose into the air and marched around him. Water was streaming down her face and hair as she walked away, toward the house.

"I think you made her mad," one of the older children said.

"I think you're right," he answered as they all started to follow her.

"You ought to talk to Pa about that. He's always good at calming Mama down when she gets upset."

Bobby looked at the boy thoughtfully, then nodded. "You may just have a good idea, there, uh. . .what's your name?"

"Thomas Jr., sir. Everyone calls me T.J."

"All right, T.J. Let's go find your pa."

He had some other things he wanted to discuss with Thomas also. The man had been married for eighteen years, so he obviously knew more than Bobby did about marriage!

But before he could do anything, he had to get out of his wet clothes. Looking around at the children, he knew he wasn't the only one. One by one, they all sloshed into the house.

fourteen

An hour or so later, everyone was fed and dry. Bobby, Thomas, and the male children were in the living room, while Susannah, Ruby, and the girls were in the kitchen— peeling potatoes and snapping beans.

Susannah had been so mad at Bobby that she hadn't spoken to him at all during breakfast. But that had worn off, and worry replaced the anger.

She never did get a chance to ask Bobby what he intended to do about their marriage once they got back to Springton. Oh, Susannah knew that worrying wasn't going to accomplish anything but more worry, but she just couldn't shake it. She never was a very patient person, and all this uncertainty was really wearing on her.

"Don't worry about your little incident, Susannah. He didn't mean to laugh at you. And he did say he was sorry," Ruby told her, looking at her with motherly concern.

Susannah shook her head. "I'm not upset about that, Ruby. It's something else. You see, things aren't exactly as they appear to be with Bobby and me. I'm afraid I've messed things up but good between us."

Ruby looked confused. "What do you mean?"

Susannah looked at Ruby's kind face and knew that she could trust her.

She narrated the whole sordid story to her. The mother of nine seemed to really listen to her and to sympathize.

"I guess I just need some advice, Ruby. I know Bobby

believes now that I had nothing to do with Beth being kidnapped by my father, and I know he isn't going to leave me in Charleston. But that's it. I don't know if he wants to give our marriage another try or. . .or get a divorce." As she said the last word, she broke down and began to cry.

Ruby put a comforting arm around her, stuffing a handkerchief in Susannah's hand. "There, there, child. Bobby Aaron seems like an honorable man to me and a good Christian one, too. I don't think he'd break his vows and do something drastic like that."

Susannah sniffed and wiped her eyes. "You don't?"

"Of course not. But I can tell you what might help, if you don't mind an older woman sticking her nose into your affairs."

"Oh, Ruby, I would love some advice. I just don't know *what* to do!"

Ruby patted her back. "Well, then, the first thing you have to do is show him that you are a good person and someone that he can trust."

"But. . .how?" She picked up a bean and absently snapped it in two.

Ruby picked up a potato. "Just love him, Susannah. Show him by your actions that you are the kind of wife that he needs. Support him, fuss over him, and then give him some room. You don't want to worry him with questions on what he plans to do. You'll know soon enough." She put down the potato and looked off into space with a dreamy expression. "There are so many special little things that you can do. A smile, a touch on the hand to let him know you're near, and even a meaningful look thrown in at just the right moment."

Susannah nodded. "I guess screeching at him like an old crow wasn't on that list, was it?"

"Oh, that doesn't matter. He feels bad for laughing at you, so why don't you tell him that you're not mad at him. Laugh about it with him. You know, the most important part about a relationship is knowing when to compromise. When a couple loves one another enough to let go of their anger and let an unimportant matter drop, you just grow closer and stronger."

"I think I understand. I need to show Bobby that I really love him."

"That's right. Let him see that you love him so much that he will want to do anything he can to make the marriage work."

Susannah was silent for a moment. "I have a hard time not worrying over everything. I've been known to be impatient and ask way too many questions. I tend to talk way more than I should."

"Oh, you don't have to stop talking. Just don't nag him to death," Ruby answered with a laugh.

Susannah laughed with her. Then, after they'd become quiet again, she asked, "You really think it will work?"

Ruby patted Susannah on her hand. "It certainly can't hurt. And God will work things out. He always does."

Susannah smiled. "That I do know. I've done more praying in the last year than I've ever done, and God has taken care of me."

"And we need to take care of these chowder peas! Who wants to help me shell?" she announced as she picked up a large bowl and set it on the counter.

A round of groans was her answer, but the girls quickly began to shell the peas.

❧

While Susannah had been pouring out her story, Bobby Joe was doing the same with Thomas. Only his version was a lot shorter and right to the point.

His question, however, was the same. "Thomas, I guess what I want to ask you is, how can I make this marriage work? I mean, we didn't even have a good beginning. I married her for selfish reasons, and now this whole fiasco with her father feels like another wall that's been slammed down to separate us."

"Hmm," Thomas said thoughtfully. "It sounds to me like you need a fresh start."

Bobby nodded. "But how?"

"Well, why don't you begin by courting her?"

Bobby sat up in his chair. "But we're already married!"

"Ah, but that's the trick. I've learned that a woman wants to keep on being courted even after you've got the ring on her finger," he told him, nodding his head as if he were dispensing a well-kept secret.

"You're kidding!" Bobby exclaimed. Then he nodded his head. "Come to think of it, my first wife always liked it when I brought her flowers and such. I just never thought it mattered so much."

"Believe me, it does. But since you've never really courted her, you need to start, and start soon if you're going to make this work. You need to let her know that you want a relationship with her. If you start courting her, that'll be a surefire way of letting her know."

"I do want it to work. When we started off on this trip, I was dead set against it and told her so. But that was just anger talking. I thought that she'd broken our trust by keeping that secret. I've been able to see her side of things a little better lately."

"Well, that's good. It's not always easy to understand the workings of a woman's mind. That's something that we men will never fully accomplish!" Thomas told him wisely.

"I guess our only consolation is that they don't understand us, either!" Bobby said with satisfaction.

Thomas just shook his head at the younger man. "Ah, but see, they think they do, which can be almost as bad."

❧

That afternoon the rain began to slow, then finally it stopped altogether. But it was still messy outside, and Susannah and Bobby wouldn't be able to leave until the next morning.

And that would give Susannah all the time she needed to execute her "plan." Ruby had taken her into her bedroom and then opened an old trunk that sat in the corner of the large room. From it she drew out several dresses, for both day and evening wear, that were all made of various shades of silk and satin. They were slightly outdated with their full skirts, but beautiful all the same.

"These are all dresses from my younger days that my father bought for me before I met my husband. I was a lot thinner then, and I think they might just fit you," Ruby explained.

Susannah fingered the fine material of one light green day dress. "Oh, they are so beautiful. They remind me a lot of my own dresses back in Charleston."

Ruby nodded toward the dresses. "Well, since you've only got your one dress, why don't you pick one of these to wear tonight, so you can dazzle that husband of yours!"

Susannah looked at Ruby with a hopeful expression. "You don't mind?"

"Oh, of course not. Let's get busy!"

When Susannah stepped out of the room, she felt like Cinderella at the prince's ball. Ruby had helped her fix her hair, lending her a pair of silver combs that held the sides of her hair back from her face. The rest of her long red tresses fell down her back.

The dress she picked was the green day dress. Its bodice had a rounded neck that was trimmed in fine ivory lace. The waist was cinched with a wide velvet ribbon, and the skirt was full, with the matching lace at the bottom. It didn't look so dated without the hoop underneath to make it stand out, and since Susannah was a little taller than Ruby, it fell to the floor at just the right length.

Oh, she'd worn fancier dresses. Every girl in Springton had commented at one time or another on the extent and beauty of her wardrobe. Susannah typically never left the house without her little white gloves, her silk fan, and her purse. No proper Southern lady would!

But Bobby's sudden travel plans didn't allow for such frivolities. She'd barely gotten away with a proper dress on at all! It *would* have to be the plainest dress she owned.

But the green dress went a long way toward making her feel better. And she couldn't wait to see what Bobby thought!

Bobby Joe and Thomas were off in the corner playing a game of checkers and didn't notice when the women walked into the room.

So Ruby cleared her throat—loudly!

Nothing. The two didn't even budge.

Ruby coughed this time. If Susannah hadn't known better, she'd think her new friend was choking.

Without so much as moving his head, Thomas called out, "Are ya okay, dear?"

Ruby exhaled a frustrated breath. "Yes, there's nothing wrong with me!"

"That's good, dear," he returned, oblivious.

Ruby looked at Susannah, and they both shrugged their shoulders. "I see that we're going to have to be a little less subtle. Come on!"

She took Susannah's arm and led her to where the men were playing. It was apparently Bobby's turn, because he kept putting his hand on a checker, then taking it off. "Thomas, honey, why don't you let Susannah play a game with Bobby," Ruby suggested.

He looked up and frowned. "We're right in the middle of a game."

Ruby put her hands on her hips and tried to communicate something with her eyes and head. She began nodding toward both Bobby and Susannah, giving her husband meaningful looks.

"Honey, is there something wrong with your head? You're not having those neck pains again, are you?" Thomas looked confused and concerned.

Ruby rolled her eyes. "Oh, for goodness sakes, Thomas!" She bent down and whispered something in his ear.

"Oh. . .oh!" he said when she was finished. He looked apologetically at Susannah. Then he said, "Uh. . .Bobby, why don't you play the rest of the game with Susannah, here. I have. . .uh. . .something that I need to take care of."

When he got up, Bobby Joe's head finally lifted and he looked at Thomas. "But we're right in the middle of a game," he protested.

"Well, I been thinking about that *discussion* we had. . . . *You* know the one," he stressed, darting his eyes meaningfully at Susannah, which made her wonder what exactly the discussion had been about! "And I thought I'd just go and see if that *thing we discussed* can be accomplished," he finished.

Bobby looked confused for a moment, then followed Thomas's gaze to where Susannah stood. He looked away, then quickly did a double-take.

"Oh, yeah," he said faintly, nodding his head. *"That* thing."

She noticed that he didn't take his eyes off of her.

Ruby and Thomas left the room, and Bobby Joe jumped up and held a chair out for her. He bent down over her shoulder as he helped her scoot the chair under the table.

"You look lovely," he said in her ear, his warm breath caressing her skin, giving her goose bumps.

She blushed as he took his chair across from her. The romantic gesture had been so unexpected and so out of character, that at first she forgot to say anything. When she saw that he was staring at her, she stammered, "Oh! Thank you." She fussed nervously with the pretty lace. "It's one of Ruby's old dresses. Mine was still damp."

He nodded, smiling at her. "I didn't even think about you not having an extra dress. I'm sorry I didn't give you enough time to pack anything."

"Oh, I don't mind. Finding Beth was on my mind more than clothes," she assured him. She then noticed that his bandage was missing.

"You've taken off your bandage!"

He nodded, touching the hair that covered the now healing wound. "Yeah. It's sore, but not bleeding. Ruby thought it needed air."

"I'm just glad that it wasn't a worse wound. I've been so worried about you."

He smiled. "I know you have. But you can stop worrying; I'm fine!" He leaned back in his chair. "Anyway, I'm just glad that we can get back on the road tomorrow. I really miss my daughter."

She saw the concern in his eyes and, remembering what Ruby had said, she reached out and touched his cheek. "We'll have her home soon, Bobby. I know we will." It was bold of her to include herself, but she wanted to let him know that she still considered herself part of the family.

And he didn't argue about it, much to her relief. Instead, he stared at her a moment, then took her hand and kissed it. "Thank you," he said gently.

Then, putting her hand down on the table, he gave her a quick wink. "Are you ready to play? I'm pretty good at this game, you know."

Following his lead, she gave him an answering smile. "Oh, really? Well, I have to warn you that I've never been beaten at this game!"

He laughed and started to reset the board. "We'll just see about that!"

Susannah's heart swelled with happiness at their playful banter. If she didn't know better, she'd think Bobby was flirting with her! But he didn't seem the type, and he'd certainly never been this way before.

Well, whatever had brought on this mood, she was going to enjoy it. And she would pray that the plan she and Ruby had hatched would work.

He was still her husband, and no matter what circumstances caused him to want to marry her, she aimed to keep him!

fifteen

The next day the Davises drove them into the small town of Wiseville. Ruby had given Susannah the pretty dress that she'd worn the night before and with it an attractive case to put her yellow dress in. Susannah had been grateful for the kindness, for they were to take the train all the way to Charleston, and it was a much better traveling garment than the plain dress she'd worn on the first leg of their trip.

After they'd said their good-byes and thank-yous to the kind family, they stopped by the sheriff's office to see if the outlaws had been found.

Sure enough, when they walked into the office, all five of the outlaws were behind bars and looking pretty upset about it.

"We were lucky. We found them before the rain started falling, thanks to some English fellow and Mr. Calhoun, the stagecoach driver," the sheriff explained. "Since there is a warrant out on 'em in North Carolina for busting out of jail, we're waiting on someone to pick them up. They'll have to deal with those charges there as well as the charges against them here for robbery and kidnapping. We've got Butch over there for attempted murder."

"Aw, we said we let her go, didn't we? Her daddy'll have us hanged if he gets wind that we kidnapped her! He liked to have done it the last time!" Durwood whined from his cell.

"Yeah, and I didn't mean to shoot 'im! He just scare't me, charging up to Dugin like a wild man. It went off in my hand, I promise!" Butch cried, adding his own defense.

Susannah looked at the pitiful expressions on the outlaws' faces and felt herself soften. Other than the inconvenience and some pain on Bobby's part, they were all right. She was sure that none of them could really shoot to kill. The reason they'd received lighter sentences in North Carolina was that half of them didn't even have bullets in their guns!

"Oh, Bobby, can't we just drop the charges of attempted murder and kidnapping? We both know they didn't *really* mean to harm us," she cooed, putting her arm through his.

"Susannah, are you out of your mind?" he burst out. But when he looked at her, his outraged expression immediately changed. He cleared his throat and began again. "I mean, Susannah, dear, they did shoot me. Don't you remember how upset you were when you thought I was dead?" His voice had undergone a major shift in tone.

Susannah stared at him and wondered what had just happened. "But they didn't. And you heard them—they didn't mean to do it. And I did sort of provoke them into taking me. You know how I can be!" she argued.

He smiled at her and patted her hand that was resting in the crook of his arm. "Susannah, of course I don't know what you mean, and besides, there's no excuse for kidnapping you."

She blinked in amazement. Did that knock to his head erase his memory? "You told me it *was* my fault! Don't you remember?"

"Uh, Ma'am?" the sheriff interrupted, embarrassed but clearly fascinated with their conversation. "No matter what the circumstances were, they did shoot your husband and kidnap you."

Susannah pulled her searching eyes from her husband. She'd just have to think about his strange behavior later. For now, she wanted to set the record straight.

"Sheriff, do I have the power to dismiss the charges against them for kidnapping me?"

"Only if your husband agrees."

Susannah looked back at Bobby. He actually smiled at her. Well, since he was in such a nice mood, she thought she might as well take advantage of it. She'd never have any peace if these men were hanged on her account.

"Bobby. . .dear," she added, copying his earlier endearment. "Please do this for me. You know in your heart of hearts that it's the right thing to do. I don't think God would want us to be so vindictive, do you?" she asked softly.

She could tell Bobby Joe was gritting his teeth in annoyance. She wondered why he didn't just tell her what was on his mind. It surely couldn't be because they were surrounded by strangers. That had never stopped him before!

"How long will they serve if I drop the charges?" Bobby finally said, resignation in his voice.

"Oh, about forty years or so."

"All right," he said to her utter amazement. "Drop the charges, sheriff."

The sheriff just shook his head, mumbling something unflattering under his breath as he made a note of Bobby's request.

In the cell behind the sheriff, all the men were on the verge of tears, thanking her for saving their miserable hides.

When they were outside and walking to the train station, Bobby Joe took her arm in a gentlemanly fashion. She looked at him and saw that he wasn't happy but for some reason was trying to hide it.

She wanted to demand that he tell her what was wrong, but then she remembered Ruby's words. She could talk, but not nag.

She sighed. How would she ever figure out what was

wrong if she didn't confront him about it?

But she wouldn't. She was supposed to let him know how much she loved him and cared for him. And he obviously was making an effort to get along, too. At least she thought that was what he was trying to do.

So she leaned into him slightly, linking both of her arms through his. "Thank you, Bobby. I know you didn't have to do it, but I appreciate your dropping those charges. They're really not evil men, just a little misguided. Maybe while they're in jail, we can have a preacher sent to talk to them."

She looked up at his strong, handsome face at the same moment he looked down at her. His light blue eyes were so clear in the morning sun as they gazed into her own. There was tenderness there, and something more, too, though Susannah was afraid to call it love.

She knew that her own love for him had to be shining in her eyes. Her heart ached to be able to freely share her feelings and have them returned.

"You're welcome, Red," he answered warmly, then glanced away. "I want you to be happy. If keeping a few outlaws from hanging will make that happen, then I'm willing to do it."

But why? she wanted to ask. Did he want this because he loved her or because he was just trying to make amends?

She wouldn't find out immediately, though.

Bobby Joe bought them passage on the train, and then they were led to a private compartment. It was quite lovely, with its rich red velvet interior and its gold-fringed trim on the shades at the windows.

They stored their two small cases and then sat across from each other. They didn't talk much, each seemingly occupied by his or her own thoughts.

Susannah was looking out the window, gazing at the lush

green forest that they were passing through when Bobby spoke to her.

"Have you ever wanted children of your own, Susannah?"

The question was so out of the blue that for a moment she didn't answer. "Uh. . .children?" Her mind raced, wondering how she should answer this. She thought about being evasive, but decided that too many secrets had been kept between them.

So she answered truthfully. "Yes, Bobby. I've always dreamed of having children. Several, in fact. That's why I love being a schoolteacher. It's the next best thing, I guess."

He stared at her so intensely that she regretted being so frank. Maybe that wasn't what he wanted to hear.

"Yet you were willing to give up that dream to marry me?" His voice was soft, but there was an underlying urgency that baffled her.

"Well, I knew that I would have Beth, and I guess, deep inside, I had hoped. . ." But she couldn't finish the sentence.

But he wasn't satisfied. "You hoped what?"

She shook her head, giving him a feeble smile. "Oh, nothing. It was just silly."

He reached across for her hand and engulfed it in his own callused hand. "Your hopes aren't silly to me, Susannah."

She swallowed, looking down at their linked hands. Without thinking, she placed her other hand on top of his strong, manly one, caressing it gently. "I hoped. . ."—she took a breath and willed herself to just say the truth—"I had hoped that you would change your mind," she whispered, her lids drifting back up slowly so she could look him fully in the face.

A range of powerful emotions crossed his face. "I'm sorry, Red. . . ," he began, but she suddenly cut him off.

Horrified by his apology, she took her hands from his. "No, no, I'm sorry. I shouldn't have admitted that. Our marriage was strictly a convenient arrangement and I had no business hoping that it could be. . ."

He stopped her by placing a thumb over her lips. Humor was brimming in his blue eyes. "Red, that's not what I was apologizing for. I'm sorry that I was so blind to your feelings, that's all. If I'd just taken a little time to get to know you the right way, I don't think I would have suggested a marriage of convenience."

She silently absorbed his words, trying not to read too much into them. "What would you have suggested?" she asked, holding her breath.

But he shook his head. "We'll get into that later. For now, I would like us to try to get to know one another better. And speaking of which. . ." He reached inside his jacket and pulled out a small package.

"For me?" she asked breathlessly.

He nodded. "I ran to the little store while you were waiting for the train. It isn't much," he said with a shrug.

She held the package with delight. "Oh, it is to me! I love it!"

"Susannah, you haven't even opened it!" he told her with a chuckle.

She beamed a radiant smile at him. "But it's from you— that's all that matters."

He gave her a wry look. "I'll remember that next time and just get you an empty package," he joked. "Now, are you going to open it?"

"Okay, okay!" She opened the brown wrapping carefully, and when she could see inside, she cried, "Oh, it's beautiful!"

He smiled proudly at her as she pulled the silk fan from the wrapping and unfolded it. The sides were made of ivory and the silk was patterned with beautiful magnolia blossoms.

"Oh, Bobby! Thank you so much. How did you know that I would want one?" she asked as she tenderly touched the intricate carving on the ivory.

He gave a self-conscious shrug. "I've never seen you without one. And I can always tell when you're aggravated about something, because you'll whip it out and start rapidly fanning yourself," he teased.

"Oh, you!" she exclaimed. "Well, if that's the case, I would figure you'd just as soon not know when I'm aggravated! But it was sweet of you all the same."

"I don't need the fan to be able to know your feelings, Red. Not anymore. And besides, I wanted to get you something to make you feel special."

She looked up at him and blurted, "But why?"

He leaned forward and took her chin in his hand, his thumb rubbing along her jaw. "Because that's what a man does when he courts a woman."

She could suddenly feel her heart pounding in her chest, and she felt her breath catch in her throat. "You're courting me?"

He grinned dryly. "If you have to ask, I must not be doing too great of a job!"

"Oh, no! You are! I just. . ." She shook her head. "We're already married," she finished, unable to put her words together.

He abruptly left his seat and sat next to her. He cradled her face with his hands. "But I didn't do things in the right order, Red. I didn't court you first. Oh, I took you around town for a few weeks and brought you to have dinner with my family, but I wasn't trying to get to know you. Not in a romantic sense, anyway." He caressed her cheek and bent to give her a soft kiss on the lips. "So I'm going to do it now."

She smiled and leaned to rub her nose against his. She loved being this close to him, loved being in his embrace. "I think I like that, Mr. Aaron," she whispered softly, her lips only a breath away from his.

"Me, too, Mrs. Aaron." Then he was kissing her. She wound her arms around his neck, and he pulled her close, deepening the kiss.

Susannah returned the kiss with every ounce of love that was in her heart. Never had he kissed her this way, and she knew that he loved her, too. It was there in his every move.

She just wished he could tell her in words!

He finally broke the kiss, and after reaching up to kiss her eyelids and nose, he hugged her tightly to him. In his arms Susannah felt so safe, so secure.

God had truly led her to this man, and although the relationship had been rocky, God was making a way for their marriage to work. He truly did make a way where there seemed to be no way, giving hope, when all she'd felt was hopelessness.

God had brought forgiveness when she thought that she'd done something unforgivable—destroyed her husband's trust with a horrible secret.

After a sweet moment, they eased away from one another, but he kept his arm around her.

"Why don't you lay your head on my shoulder and get some rest. I'll wake you for lunch."

"All right," she answered, doing as he suggested.

Suddenly she laughed softly as the pieces of the puzzle fell into place. "That's why you were acting so oddly! You weren't arguing with me because you were trying to be gallant and courtly!" she informed him, making reference to his behavior earlier.

"You thought I was acting odd?"

"Well," she said, her eyes closing, "you just weren't acting like your normal self. You know—grumpy," she teased.

She heard the rumble of his chest as he chuckled. "Well, I'm trying to reform."

She patted his chest. "Oh, don't reform too much. I like you just the way you are," she told him and then yawned.

She felt him put a tender kiss on her temple. "I'm glad. Now, quit talking and go to sleep," he ordered, though his voice was light and loving.

"Yes, sir," she murmured.

Just as she drifted off to sleep, she thought she heard him whisper, "I love you, Susannah."

But, of course, it was probably just another one of her fanciful dreams.

sixteen

Courting Susannah was something that Bobby Joe took great pleasure in doing. Just watching her eyes light up every time he did something special brought him more joy than he ever thought he would share with another woman.

He was fascinated by every aspect of Susannah as a woman, a wife, and a friend. He realized that she was loyal and worthy of his trust. She hated to hurt people's feelings and would usually go out of her way for those she loved. She didn't mind sharing her opinion, but he didn't mind that, either. She thought so differently from him that it was intriguing just to hear her point of view.

He thought about Leanna, too. But it wasn't to compare the two or to hang on to old memories. In his heart he was saying good-bye to her, forgiving her for not telling him the truth about her illness. He'd loved her as much as any young man could love his wife, but he was ready to move on to a new life with Susannah.

He was no longer the foolish young man who had been married to Leanna. He was more mature, so his feelings ran deeper, were somehow more profound. He supposed things would have developed that way for Leanna, had she lived.

But those feelings were all for Susannah now. He wanted all those children that she dreamed of. He wanted Beth to have a mother.

He wanted her love just as much as he wanted to give her his own.

They were almost to Charleston now. The conductor had made the call for the Charleston station just minutes earlier, announcing that they'd be arriving in half an hour. After they picked up Beth, Bobby Joe had something special planned.

"Thinking about Beth?" Susannah asked, breaking into his musings.

He looked down at her as she sat beside him, holding his hand. "Among other things," he answered with a mysterious smile.

She nudged him playfully. "Bobby Joe Aaron, are you the one keeping secrets now?"

He bent to give her a quick kiss. "No secret. Just a surprise."

She groaned. "Oh, you know how impatient I am! Can't you just give me a teensy-weensy little hint?"

"Not even an itty-bitty one," he said happily.

He smiled as she sighed and gave up. She didn't appear to be happy about it, but she would be.

Charleston's station was busy with activity as they stepped off the train. Together they walked through the street until they found a place to hire a conveyance to take them to her father's house.

When they were on their way, he noticed Susannah looking around, getting reacquainted with her former home.

"Do you miss living here?" he asked.

She swept the area with her keen eyes and then looked at him. "You know, I haven't thought about this place hardly at all since I moved to Springton. It's a beautiful city, but it's no longer home."

He brought her hand up to his lips. "I'm glad to hear that. It would be difficult to move our family back and forth between the two towns."

She looked at him, confused. "Do you mean that you'd

move here if I wanted to live here?"

"Red, I'd move to England if that would make you happy," he told her matter-of-factly.

Immediately her eyes filled with tears. She took a hankie from her little purse and began dabbing at her eyes. "Now, see what your being sweet to me does? It makes me cry like an infant!"

He put his arm around her and kissed the top of her head. "You want me to stop?"

"No!" she cried aloud, causing the driver to turn and stare at them for a moment. When he turned back around, they both burst out laughing.

Finally, they arrived. They stood at the gate for a moment, staring at the imposing mansion at the end of the long walkway.

"Are you ready?" he asked, lacing his fingers with hers. It gave him comfort and strength to hold her hand as he prepared himself for a battle with Susannah's father, which he worried might take place.

"Yes, I am. We've got God on our side. Remember that," she reminded him, her voice strong and unafraid.

"I will never doubt it again," he promised.

They opened the gate and began the lengthy walk to the large porch. The Butler mansion was a huge white house with four massive columns in front, set in a half-circle; the columns supported the porch, which was three stories high. Large windows stretched away on either side of the centered porch. On the roof was an octagon-shaped observatory with windows on each of its sides. Telescopes and other equipment could be seen behind the windows.

Bobby had forgotten just how big the house was. The last and only time he'd been here had been when he'd asked for

Leanna's hand. He'd been promptly thrown out. So they'd left town the next night and eloped. Bobby Joe had been there on business and had had three more days to go before he was supposed to leave, but he hadn't taken any chances. As soon as he'd placed the ring on her finger, he'd taken her away from the town and from her father.

He never dreamed he'd be back. Only for Beth would he do this. . .or for his wife. He would give his life for either of them if he had to.

The door was opened by a dour black man who wore what appeared to be a perpetual frown. He narrowed his hawklike gaze on Bobby Joe at first, sniffing disdainfully at his western attire. But when his eyes swept over Susannah, the frown disappeared and was replaced by a look of pure joy.

"Miss Susannah! Why, we have surely missed you so!" the man cried in his Deep South accent. He held open the door and stepped aside. "Come in, come in!"

"Thank you, Samuel. It's wonderful to see you, too. How's your family?" Susannah asked as they stepped into the massive foyer.

"Oh, right as rain!" Samuel responded.

"Samuel, this is my husband, Bobby Joe Aaron. Bobby, Samuel has been with our family ever since I was a little girl."

Bobby Joe shook the man's hand, noticing that he wasn't giving him any more frowns. "I can't believe our little Miss Susannah has gone and gotten herself a husband, but it surely is nice to meet you, sir."

"Samuel, we need to know if my father is home," Susannah asked.

He nodded. "Got home about two days ago, he did."

Susannah looked at Bobby and then asked, "Did he have a little girl with him?"

Both of their hearts sank as the older man shook his head. "No, Ma'am. There's no child here. Hasn't been since you and Miss Leanna were toddling around this old place."

Bobby Joe's heart sped up as panic and worry slammed his system. He hadn't anticipated that Butler wouldn't have Beth. It had never entered his mind.

Had something happened to her on the way?

"Where is he?" Bobby demanded, taking Samuel by surprise by his brisk tone.

"He's in his study. First door to your right."

"Thank you, Samuel!" Susannah called out as Bobby Joe grabbed her hand and ran down the hall, pulling her after him.

"Bobby, please calm down," Susannah pleaded, but he was beyond hearing her. He nearly knocked the door off its hinges as he entered.

In two seconds he had pulled Winston Butler from his easy chair and was holding him in front of him by the collar. "Where is she, Butler? Where is my daughter?" he barked. The hold on his rage was extremely thin. He had to concentrate on *not* hitting the old man.

"I don't know what you're talking about, you Texas cowpoke. Now let go of me!" Winston ordered, though it sounded weak. Bobby could see the fear in his eyes.

"Bobby, please don't hurt him," Susannah begged, as she pulled on his arm. "You're going to give him a heart attack!"

"Where is Beth, Winston? Tell me now, before I knock you through that window!" He shook the man to emphasize his point. Beside him, Susannah began to cry as she tugged on Bobby Joe.

"I don't have Beth! I promise!" he sputtered, clearly fearing for his life.

"Bobby, I think he's telling the truth. Please don't hurt

him," Susannah cried again, and this time her voice got to him. Taking a few deep breaths, he let the man go.

"What are you saying? Did you drop her off somewhere? Is that it?"

He watched as Susannah ran to him, smoothing out his suit jacket.

"No," Winston Butler answered. "What I'm saying is that I never had her. Are you trying to tell me that she's missing?"

Despite being upset, Bobby Joe could see that the man was telling the truth. Helplessly he looked at Susannah. Tears started to well up in her eyes again as she shook her head in disbelief.

"If you don't have her, then who does?" he asked, not really expecting an answer. In a daze, he stumbled over to a chair and sank down in it. He raked a hand through his hair and then down his face.

Susannah looked at her father. "Daddy, Beth was kidnapped the morning you left town. We both thought you had brought her here. We've been traveling for days just to get her back."

Her father's face looked pale as the import of her words seemed to sink in. "How could you think that I would ever do something like that, Susannah?" he asked sadly, clearly offended by the accusation.

"Because that's exactly what you intended!" a low, Southern voice announced from the doorway.

They all turned to see Susannah's ever-absent mother standing in the doorway. As usual, the still-beautiful woman was dressed as if she were going to a ball, with sequins decorating her burgundy gown and matching feathers in her gray-blond hair. Gloved hands were on her slim hips, and a frown curved her rouged lips.

"Mariah! What are you doing here?" Winston demanded,

obviously not pleased in the least to see his wife. "I thought you said you were staying in Paris!"

"Why, you would just love that, wouldn't you, Winston," she purred in her lazy Southern accent, as she strolled into the room. "But I just happened to come home right after you left for Texas. Jamison was the one who told me you'd intended to bring Beth home with you."

Winston's face grew blood red. "Jamison was lying!" he shouted, referring to his talkative lawyer and business partner.

"I think the only liar involved in this affair is you!" Mariah returned as she snapped her wrist to unfurl her black fan. After a few quick strokes, she walked past Winston and gave Susannah a hug.

"Hello, Susannah-Sugar. I'm not going to lie and tell you that my little old heart is not broken in two because I wasn't invited to your wedding," she said in a soothing, motherly voice.

Susannah hugged her mother back. Mariah always acted like they'd talked just the day before, even when it had been months since the last time they'd seen one another. In truth, Susannah didn't really know her. But she went along with the charade. It always seemed to please her mother.

"I'm sorry, Mama. It was all rather. . .uh. . .sudden," Susannah told her absently, wanting to get to the topic at hand. "Mama? What did you mean just now? Do you know something about all this that Bobby and I don't?"

"Yes, yes. But I'll get to that in a moment." She looked at Bobby and smiled. "You haven't introduced me to my son-in-law. I didn't get to meet him the first time he became that."

Bobby looked taken aback at her bold speech. Susannah was appalled, but not surprised. If she'd inherited anything from her mother, it seemed to be an uncontrollable tongue.

"Hello, Mrs. Butler," Bobby said warily, as he shook the gloved hand that she held out to him.

"Oh, let's not stand on ceremony! You can call me Mama!" she exclaimed with a charming smile.

Susannah had a feeling that getting information out of her mother was going to take forever. So she turned to her father. "Daddy, can you just tell us the truth? Please, Daddy. Beth means the whole world to Bobby and to me," she pleaded.

Bobby Joe came up behind her, putting a comforting hand on her shoulder. "Please, sir," he asked, his voice raspy with worry.

Winston sent his wife a scowl, but when he looked back at Susannah and Bobby Joe, he sighed. "All right, all right! I did intend to kidnap her. But when I got there, she was already gone!"

"Oh, Daddy!" Susannah exclaimed with a disappointed cry.

"Well, I was just doing what I thought was right for this family!" he defended.

Bobby Joe briefly put his head against Susannah's. "It doesn't matter. We still don't know who took her."

"Oh, but *I* do."

All three pairs of eyes turned to look at Mariah Butler. For a second or two, no one said a word.

Then Bobby snapped into action. "You know who took her? Then why didn't you say so, when—"

"Oh, calm down!" Mariah scolded, waving her hand at him as if shooing him away. "*I* took her, of course," she stated calmly.

And before anyone could say anything, she called over her shoulder for her maid to bring her granddaughter in.

Right there in front of their eyes, both Bobby Joe and Susannah knew they were witnessing a miracle from God.

Beth walked into the room, holding the maid's hand. Her mouth was spread wide in a smile.

"Daddy! Mama!" Beth called out before running to them. Bobby swept her up in his arms and then opened up one arm to include Susannah in the embrace.

When they'd finished their hugs and kisses, the three of them sat down to talk, momentarily forgetting that the elder Butlers were in the room.

But Mariah was not one to be ignored for long.

"Well, now that we've gotten that hullabaloo out of the way, I think it's a good time to tell you that Winston and I will be moving back to Texas with you," she announced proudly, folding her arms across her chest.

"What do you mean 'Winston and I'?" Winston Butler demanded, getting all flustered again. "You're not dragging me off to that backward, lawless land!"

"Don't shout, Sugar. You're going to give yourself a heart attack." She walked over to sit beside her daughter.

"I've been attending revival meetings in Paris, and I recently accepted Christ. I know now that I have been a terrible mother to you, Susannah, and I want to try to make it up to you." Susannah could see a tear gleaming in her mother's light green eyes.

Susannah couldn't believe what her mother was saying. Nearly all her life she'd prayed that her parents would become Christians, but she wondered if she would ever see it happen. Now she could see a real difference in her mother— there was a tenderness in her eyes that had been absent before.

"Oh, that's wonderful, Mama! I've always prayed that you would." She hugged her mother again.

"I know, Sugar." She pulled back and then looked at a

confused Winston. "That's also why I want to make a go of our marriage, Winston. We were both so upset that our parents arranged our marriage, that we never really tried to get to know one another, did we?" She got up and walked to him. "And when I didn't have a son, like I always thought you wanted, I ran away. But I'm sorry I did that. I would like to try to make our marriage work."

Winston shook his head, then suddenly pulled Mariah into his arms. "You foolish woman. I never did care about that. I thought you left because you couldn't stand the sight of me."

Susannah sat there, staring wide-eyed at the incredible scene being played out before them. "If I wasn't seeing this, I wouldn't believe it!" she whispered to Bobby.

Bobby Joe looked at her over Beth's head and smiled. "God does work in mysterious ways! Looks like He's giving your parents a second chance!"

"But do they need to come to Texas to do that?" she asked with exasperation in her voice. And she said it a little too loudly.

"Oh, pooh! Don't you worry your little head about us, Susannah Sugar. We're just going to be one big, happy family!" She looked at Bobby Joe. "Bobby, I'm sure you have an extra room or two for us to stay in while we build us something, don't you?"

Susannah put her head down and groaned.

seventeen

That next morning, Susannah and Beth waited at the train station alone. Bobby Joe had told them to wait for him while he ran an errand.

Susannah couldn't think of what errand he could possibly have to run in Charleston, so she guessed that this must have something to do with the surprise he'd told her about.

But when he returned, it was time to board the train, so she didn't get a chance to ask him. Unfortunately, they were unable to get a private compartment, although they did sit together, Bobby sitting across from Beth and Susannah, as they made their way home.

When they'd gotten settled and the train had begun to roll, Susannah was hoping that he'd tell her what he'd been doing, but he just smiled at them and settled back in his seat.

She supposed they'd just have to wait.

Beth had a small slate and some chalk and was drawing pictures of flowers. She seemed to be unaffected by her trip with her grandmother. Susannah's mother had made their being together seem like a big adventure, so Beth hadn't been afraid that she might never see her father again. Mariah had assured her that they'd only be traveling for a few days and that her daddy would come and get her. How she knew that, Susannah wasn't sure. Mariah's thoughts ran so differently from those of everyone else!

But they were all together now, and Susannah had high hopes that they would remain together. She would have a better idea if Bobby would only talk to her about it!

She looked across and found him staring at her. She was going to glance away, but found that she couldn't. Something precious, something truly beautiful, passed between them as they gazed into one another's eyes. It was all she'd ever hoped for since the day she'd met him.

He was looking at her with so much love that she believed she could feel it. It didn't matter that he didn't say the words. He would do so eventually.

He leaned forward and took her hands. "Aren't you going to ask me where I went this morning?" he teased, his eyes gleaming with humor.

"Now, you know I'm trying to be good, Bobby Joe Aaron. It's not fair for you to bait me!" she scolded playfully, as she pulled on his hands. "But you know I'm just bursting to find out!"

He laughed and kissed her knuckles. "Well, I had something planned when I thought we'd be able to get a private compartment," he explained. "I went out this morning to get you something special, something I should have given you in the first place."

"Oh, Bobby, can't you just give it to me? Who cares if we're not alone."

He sat back and thought a moment. Then he looked all about them and stood up. He took something out of his pocket, and then, to her utter amazement, he dropped down to one knee, right there in the aisle, beside her seat.

"Bobby! What. . .?" she started to whisper, as she noticed that everyone had begun to look at them.

Beth exclaimed, "Daddy, whatcha doing down there?"

"Shh!" He smiled and cleared his throat. "I have something that I want to ask Susannah," he told her, her face solemn and sincere.

"Hey, looky there! He's going to propose!" a loud voice with a country twang sang out, causing the whole car to erupt in laughter.

Normally Bobby Joe would have scowled at everyone for intruding on his business, but this time he shook his head and chuckled.

"Susannah, I know that I've asked you this before, but I did it the wrong way and for all the wrong reasons." He held up a beautiful gold ring set with three good-sized diamonds. She gasped as he slid the ring on her finger next to her wedding band.

"Susannah, I love you with all my heart, and I'd be the happiest man in the world if you'd marry me."

Susannah's eyes filled with tears as the words that she'd longed to hear poured over her like a soothing balm. She put her other hand on his cheek and was about to answer yes when Beth called out loudly, "But you already married her once, Daddy!"

Laughter erupted again, and Susannah knew her face was glowing a bright red.

"That's right, sweetheart. But I didn't do it so well the first time, so I thought I'd try again!"

The woman sitting across the aisle from them slapped her husband on the shoulder and snapped, "Why don't you ever say romantic things like that to me?"

"Well, if I hankered down on one knee like he's a-doin', I'm liable to throw my back out!" he returned.

Susannah and Bobby laughed at the antics of the crowd around them. They all seemed to enjoy the spectacle Bobby was making.

Imagine that, she thought with wonder. *The remote Bobby Joe Aaron on his knees in the middle of a bunch of strangers, asking me to remarry him. God surely must have a sense of humor!*

Beth leaned over Susannah's lap to get a closer look at the ring. "Ooowee! That's a pretty ring, Mama!"

"It sure is, Beth," she whispered, keeping her eyes trained on her adoring husband.

"Well, ain'tcha goin' to give the man an answer?" someone called out.

"Yeah! Are you going to marry him or not?"

Bobby Joe raised his eyebrows. "Yeah, Red. What's the answer going to be?"

She laughed out loud and yelled, "Yes!" Bobby Joe whooped for joy as he got up, taking Susannah with him. Then, right there in front of the passengers on the train bound to Texas, Bobby kissed Susannah. Whistles and clapping were heard all around them.

"But y'all are already married!" Beth said again, giggling at the sight of her daddy kissing in public.

⟡

The ride after the proposal was a lot more peaceful and uneventful than it had started out being. Of course, Susannah had to fill everyone in on what they'd just been through, because the passengers were all brimming with curiosity about why Susannah and Bobby Joe would remarry!

At last, after days of traveling, they finally reached their destination. For some reason Bobby Joe had pulled down the window shade and had made Susannah promise to leave it there.

When she asked him why, he just asked her to trust him. That just made her more curious, but she complied. She couldn't imagine what else he had up his sleeve.

All Susannah knew for sure was that they were going to

be a real family. She and Bobby Joe had even talked about having more children.

She felt as if God had just poured out a bucket of blessings on her all at once. She didn't know when it had happened for Bobby, but he'd really let go of all his anger and bitterness toward her and the rest of her family. He no longer was irritable and grumpy. In fact, he was now happy, carefree, and so charming! She had always known he had the potential to be this way, but she had wondered if she'd ever see it.

With God, all things were indeed possible.

And as for herself, she'd learned a valuable lesson in trust. She hadn't told Bobby her secret because she hadn't trusted God to work things out. She thought that she could control it all on her own. But secrets are never buried forever. Sooner or later they will come out and bite you!

And God had given all of them, including Beth, each other because He knew they all needed to be loved. Susannah needed to be loved as a wife and mate, Bobby Joe needed someone to love him through his hurts, to restore to him all that he'd lost, and Beth needed the love of a mother.

God had provided miracles for all of them, including her parents. Though she was still a little overwhelmed by the fact that her parents were reconciling and moving to Texas, she was grateful that God was working in her family.

"This's it!" Bobby said from beside her as he bent down to grab their bags. "Are y'all ready?"

Susannah and Beth both nodded tiredly as they walked down the aisle and down the steps to the station boardwalk.

They were making their way around the station, when Susannah saw them. Nearly the whole town was standing out in the middle of Main Street. . .waiting for them. Flower petals were being flung all over the streets, and everyone was dressed in their best Sunday suits.

"What in the world?" she gasped as she looked at the scene before her.

"I wired ahead and asked Patience and my brothers to set this up," Bobby whispered in her ear.

Silently she let him lead her forward into the waiting crowd as they all started greeting them, wishing them a happy marriage.

"Susannah!" Patience called out as she ran toward her, Rachel in tow. "I have your wedding dress all ready for you at Rachel's house. Let's hurry so we can begin the ceremony!"

Bobby handed her over to the women, and all she could do was shake her head and babble, "Wedding dress?"

"Oh, you poor thing, he wanted to surprise you," Patience explained, putting her arm around her. "He wired me a couple of days ago and asked me to put together a big wedding so you two could say your vows again. Why, I can't tell you how it put my mind at ease, knowing that you'd worked out your differences!"

Rachel led her into her house. "I thought we were going to have to send you the book that Patience read to help her get the sheriff's attention! What was it called?"

Patience rolled her eyes. "Oh, *that* book! It was called *Emma Hadley's Young Ladies Guide to Courtship and Marriage*, or something like that! I read in that book that men like it when you bat your eyelashes at them. Well, I went around doing that for weeks, and all that time Lee thought I had something wrong with my eyes!" She laughed. "Believe me, it would have done Susannah more harm than good!"

Susannah finally found her tongue as they ushered her into Rachel's bedroom. "I can't believe this is happening! I mean, we did this not five weeks ago!"

Rachel pushed her down into a chair and began combing out her hair. "Yes, but you're happy this time. I knew something was wrong the first time, but you seemed so determined to go through with it."

"I know. I just loved him so much," she explained.

Patience took down the wedding dress that Susannah had worn the first time and was smoothing out the wrinkles. "We knew that, too. And that's why I didn't say more to you. I knew that Bobby would realize he loves you, too. He needed someone to love him, to help deal with his hurts."

While they dressed her, Susannah told them all that had happened during the trip to and from Charleston. They thought the whole thing was wildly romantic, and they said they wished they had been on the train when Bobby proposed!

After she was dressed, they led her outside to the back of the church, where everyone was assembled. Flowers were strung everywhere, and a flower-clad arch had been built where they were to stand. Folks were sitting on the grass or on chairs they'd brought from home, ready to witness the ceremony.

It was like a dreamland, with the warm breeze and the music of a variety of birds singing, as they sat under the big oak trees that shaded the yard. There in the archway stood her husband, and this time she didn't have to guess how he felt about her, for his eyes were full of love and anticipation.

Susannah looked at her best friends, and they kissed her on the cheek. Then both of them walked down the "aisle," a pathway created by the people who had moved aside to let them pass. Rachel and Patience were acting as Susannah's bridesmaids. She smiled when she realized that she hadn't even asked them to stand up with her!

Beth ran up to her. "Mama! Can I be a bridesmaid, too?" she asked, excited and looking all grown up in her pretty dress. Susannah had no idea where Beth had changed clothes!

"Of course you can, but you better hurry!" She patted her

on the back, then her stepdaughter skipped down the path that the others had taken.

It was then that she noticed that Billy Ray, Daniel, and Tommy were standing as groomsmen beside their big brother. All three noticed her looking at them and waved. Tommy even called out hello before he was cut short when Daniel stomped on his foot.

She realized that everyone had turned to look at her, so she started to walk down the path to her husband; suddenly a hand on her arm stopped her short.

"Now you hold on right there, little girl! You got married without us last time, and we aren't going to let it happen again!" her father exclaimed gruffly as he rested his hands on the lapels of his black suit.

"That's right, Sugar! I even brought you a bouquet of roses." Mariah handed her daughter a beautiful array of white roses and kissed her on the cheek. "Now close your mouth, Sugar, before you collect flies, and let's start walking. Folks are waiting!"

Susannah closed her mouth and let both of them lead her down the path. "How did you. . .?"

"We were on the same train as you but in a private compartment. Bobby told us to stay out of sight so we could surprise you," Mariah explained as she smiled and nodded to everyone as they passed by them. Even as she escorted her daughter down the path, she was a social butterfly.

"But Bobby told me there weren't any more private compartments," Susannah whispered.

"Of course not, Sugar! We took the last one."

They had made it to the reverend and Bobby by then. Her parents gave her away to him, and Bobby took her hand and held it tight.

This time their vows were spoken with so much love that every woman was crying by the time it was over.

Finally, Brother Caleb announced, "I now pronounce you husband and wife. . .again!" A scatter of laughter went through the audience.

Beth apparently didn't like being left out, because she started pulling on Brother Caleb's coat. "You forgot me!" she complained.

"Okay, I pronounce you husband, wife, and daughter!"

The crowd cheered and then waited because Brother Caleb next announced that Bobby was to kiss his bride!

Bobby kissed her gently and reverently, putting his hands on either side of her face. She smiled at him as they broke apart and rubbed noses with him, making the crowd chuckle.

"Ladies and gentlemen," Brother Caleb announced to the crowd, "I present to you Mr., Mrs., and Daughter Aaron!" He winked at Beth as he said the last, and she winked back.

But Bobby didn't go anywhere. He pulled his wife to him again and kissed her soundly. Then he pulled back only a fraction, their lips just a breath apart.

"I love you, Red," he told her softly, for her ears only, as he looked deeply into her eyes.

"And I love you, Bobby. Forever," she added.

"Forever," he agreed, and kissed her again.

Every female in the place sighed as they watched the touching scene. Sure, it was strange that they were getting married again only a month after they'd done it the first time. But somehow it also was so very romantic.

No one knew what Bobby Joe and Susannah had really been through, not even their friends. No one was aware that their love was more than romantic—it was a miracle from God.

But no one needed to know.

It was *their* little secret.

A Letter To Our Readers

Dear Reader:

In order that we might better contribute to your reading enjoyment, we would appreciate your taking a few minutes to respond to the following questions. We welcome your comments and read each form and letter we receive. When completed, please return to the following:

Rebecca Germany, Fiction Editor
Heartsong Presents
PO Box 719
Uhrichsville, Ohio 44683

1. Did you enjoy reading *Susannah's Secret?*
   ☐ Very much. I would like to see more books
      by this author!
   ☐ Moderately
      I would have enjoyed it more if _____
      _____
      _____

2. Are you a member of **Heartsong Presents**?   Yes ☐ No ☐
   If no, where did you purchase this book?_____
   _____

3. How would you rate, on a scale from 1 (poor) to 5 (superior), the cover design?_____

4. On a scale from 1 (poor) to 10 (superior), please rate the following elements.

   _____ Heroine   _____ Plot

   _____ Hero   _____ Inspirational theme

   _____ Setting   _____ Secondary characters

5. These characters were special because _____

   _____

   _____

6. How has this book inspired your life? _____

   _____

   _____

7. What settings would you like to see covered in future **Heartsong Presents** books? _____

   _____

   _____

8. What are some inspirational themes you would like to see treated in future books? _____

   _____

   _____

9. Would you be interested in reading other **Heartsong Presents** titles?   Yes ☐   No ☐

10. Please check your age range:
    ☐ Under 18   ☐ 18-24   ☐ 25-34
    ☐ 35-45   ☐ 46-55   ☐ Over 55

11. How many hours per week do you read? _____

Name _____

Occupation _____

Address _____

City _____ State _____ Zip _____

British COLUMBIA

The early twentieth century not only births the town of Dawson Creek, British Columbia, but changes it from a prairie village into the southern anchor of the Alcan Highway. Follow the fictionalized growth of author Janelle Burnham Schneider's hometown through the eyes of characters who hold onto hopes, dreams. . .and love.

This captivating volume combines four complete novels of inspiring love that you'll treasure.

paperback, 464 pages, 5 ¾₆" x 8"

❤ ❤ ❤ ❤ ❤ ❤ ❤ ❤ ❤ ❤ ❤ ❤ ❤ ❤

❤ ❤ ❤ ❤ ❤ ❤ ❤ ❤ ❤ ❤ ❤ ❤ ❤ ❤

·········Presents·········

Hearts♥ng Presents
Love Stories Are Rated G!

That's for godly, gratifying, and of course, great! If you love a thrilling love story, but don't appreciate the sordidness of some popular paperback romances, **Heartsong Presents** is for you. In fact, **Heartsong Presents** is the *only inspirational romance book club* featuring love stories where Christian faith is the primary ingredient in a marriage relationship.

Sign up today to receive your first set of four, never before published Christian romances. Send no money now; you will receive a bill with the first shipment. You may cancel at any time without obligation, and if you aren't completely satisfied with any selection, you may return the books for an immediate refund!

Imagine. . .four new romances every four weeks—two historical, two contemporary—with men and women like you who long to meet the one God has chosen as the love of their lives. . . all for the low price of $9.97 postpaid.

To join, simply complete the coupon below and mail to the address provided. **Heartsong Presents** romances are rated G for another reason: They'll arrive *Godspeed!*